PUFFIN

THE BULLY BOYS

ERIC WALTERS is the highly acclaimed and best-selling author of over seventy-five novels for children and young adults. His novels have won the Silver Birch Award and the Red Maple Award, as well as numerous other prizes, including the White Pine, Snow Willow, Tiny Torgi, Ruth Schwartz, and IODE Violet Downey Book Awards, and have received honours from the Canadian Library Association Book Awards, the Canadian Children's Book Centre, and UNESCO's international award for Literature in Service of Tolerance.

To find out more about Eric and his novels, or to arrange for him to speak at your school, visit his website at www.ericwalters.net.

ALSO BY ERIC WALTERS
FROM PENGUIN

Benjamin,
Ride with

THE
BULLY
BOYS.

ERIC WALTERS

This novel is dedicated to James FitzGibbon.
Without his bravery and daring there
would not have been a Canada.

PUFFIN
an imprint of Penguin Canada

Published by the Penguin Group
Penguin Group (Canada), 90 Eglinton Avenue East, Suite 700, Toronto, Ontario, Canada M4P 2Y3
(a division of Pearson Canada Inc.)

Penguin Group (USA) Inc., 375 Hudson Street, New York, New York 10014, U.S.A.
Penguin Books Ltd, 80 Strand, London WC2R 0RL, England
Penguin Ireland, 25 St Stephen's Green, Dublin 2, Ireland (a division of Penguin Books Ltd)
Penguin Group (Australia), 250 Camberwell Road, Camberwell, Victoria 3124, Australia
(a division of Pearson Australia Group Pty Ltd)
Penguin Books India Pvt Ltd, 11 Community Centre, Panchsheel Park, New Delhi – 110 017, India
Penguin Group (NZ), 67 Apollo Drive, Rosedale, Auckland 0632, New Zealand
(a division of Pearson New Zealand Ltd)
Penguin Books (South Africa) (Pty) Ltd, 24 Sturdee Avenue, Rosebank, Johannesburg 2196, South Africa

Penguin Books Ltd, Registered Offices: 80 Strand, London WC2R 0RL, England

First published in Viking hardcover by Penguin Canada, a division of Pearson Canada Inc., 2000.
Published in Puffin paperback by Penguin Canada, a division of Pearson Canada Inc., 2001, 2008.

Published in this edition, 2012

2 3 4 5 6 7 8 9 10 (WEB)

LIBRARY AND ARCHIVES CANADA CATALOGUING IN PUBLICATION

Walters, Eric, 1957–
The bully boys / Eric Walters.

ISBN 978-0-14-318384-6

1. Canada—History—War of 1812—Juvenile fiction. 2. FitzGibbon, James, 1780–1863—Juvenile fiction.
3. Beaver Dams (Thorold, Ont.), Battle of, 1813—Juvenile fiction. I. Title.

PS8595.A598B84 2012   jC813'.54   C2012-900951-2

Visit the Penguin Canada website at www.penguin.ca

Special and corporate bulk purchase rates available; please see
www.penguin.ca/corporatesales or call 1-800-810-3104, ext. 2477.

ALWAYS LEARNING   **PEARSON**

CHAPTER ONE

JULY 1813

PIIIIINNNGGG! the bell rang out as I opened the door to the general store. I stepped inside, and it called out again as I closed the door behind me.

I was amazed by what I saw. Once the store had been overflowing with an assortment of dry goods. Then, little by little, the items had started to leave the shelves, not to be replaced. Now there were mainly empty spaces.

"Hello!" I called out. There was no answer and no sign of anybody. I walked between the empty shelves toward the counter at the rear of the store.

"Hello!" I shouted again.

The curtain at the back parted and old Mr. McCann pushed through.

"Who's there!" he growled, waving his cane in the air.

"It's just me, Mr. McCann," I answered.

"Thomas?" he asked.

"Yes, sir."

He stopped, smiled and pulled his spectacles out of his pocket.

"Sorry, I thought it might be soldiers."

There were over three thousand American soldiers stationed at Fort George near our village of Queenston. They'd streamed across the Niagara River that spring, forcing the badly outnumbered Canadian and British troops to retreat and abandon this part of Canadian soil—at least for now. Mostly the Americans stayed inside the walls of the fort and left us alone, but sometimes they'd sent patrols through the countryside and villages from here to Niagara Falls.

"It's good to see you, son," old man McCann said as he slowly made his way across the floor.

I couldn't believe how much he'd aged in the few weeks since the Americans had taken over the fort. My Ma had said it was from both the work and the worry—

work around the store now that he was left on his own to run things, and worry about where his son was fighting and what he was doing now.

I understood the worry. I was worried about my Pa. He was with the militia, along with my uncle, whose family farmed the parcel of land next to ours. Most all of the men from the area, including Mr. McCann's son, had volunteered to fight alongside the British redcoats. They were part of the force that had had to retreat when the Americans came. I'd heard, but I didn't know for sure, that they had all been pulled back to Stoney Creek, or maybe to Burlington Bay. Of course those were all rumours and didn't mean much of anything. My Ma said that sometimes rumours are true and sometimes they're deliberately started to try and fool the enemy, so I shouldn't believe much of what I heard.

If I'd been a year older . . . or maybe two . . . I wouldn't have needed to guess because I'd have been right there beside them. It didn't seem fair that just because I was only fourteen I wasn't allowed to join. I was as big as a lot of those men—bigger than some—and I could shoot straighter than almost anybody around these parts. But I was stuck on the farm, missing out on the adventure. Instead of helping to drive those Americans back across the border I was driving a plough horse back and forth across the fields.

It was strange with Pa gone. But I guess no stranger than it was for any of the farms up and down the Niagara. All the men were gone. All that was left were women and old men like Mr. McCann and children . . . and of course a few like me who weren't children but still weren't thought of as men.

Of course now, with both my Pa and uncle gone away, I had to work the farm like I was a grown man. I'd never worked so hard in my life. It wasn't that I minded hard work—growing up on a farm you get used to it. Me, my cousin who was twelve, and my thirteen-year-old brother, who was nearly as big as me, did everything that needed to be done on both farms. My little sister Sarah helped too, mainly by caring for the twins so Ma could do other things. As hard as I worked, Ma and Auntie Lizzie worked harder. Ma was working when I got up in the morning and still at it when I turned in for the night.

"How's your family doing, laddie?" Mr. McCann asked.

"Everybody's fine."

"Aye, that's good to hear."

"And how are things here?" I asked hesitantly.

"We're getting by as best we can. But I'm a mite long in the tooth to be doing this job now. What with my daughter-in-law so busy with the children and the new baby, there isn't much choice but to have me work, now is there?"

"I guess not," I answered.

Old Mr. McCann was the one who'd started up the store in the beginning, long, long before I was born, even before my Pa and his brother had settled their claims. When I was really small he was always behind the counter working. But after his son took over, a few years ago, Mr. McCann didn't have to do much more than putter around and help.

"So what brings you to the store this morning, Thomas?"

"We need a few things," I said pulling a list out from my pocket. "But there . . . there . . . isn't much . . ."

"Pretty empty isn't it?" he asked.

I nodded. It didn't feel right to take anything when there was so little left.

"Not much is arriving these days, and what I get is taken by those darn American soldiers."

"They buy their supplies from you?" I asked in amazement. No wonder his shelves were so empty.

"Ha! Steal is what they do! They just come in and take what they want. Some of them throw down a few coins, not near worth what they take, and then leave again."

"I'm sorry . . . I'm sure we can get by . . . I'll just tell my Ma that there weren't any—"

"You'll tell your mother nothing," he interrupted, taking the list from my hand. "You'll just give her what she asked for."

"But—"

"But nothing." He paused and gave me a smile. "I have some things put away. I'll be back in a while." He limped off through the curtain to the storeroom, leaving me alone.

I walked over to the counter. The glass jars that used to hold sticks of candy were empty. Those peppermint sticks always made our trips to the store so special. Even when money was scarce there was always a halfpence to buy a piece of candy each for me and my brothers and sisters—and a piece for Pa, too. Ma always kidded Pa about his sweet tooth.

Piiiiinnnggg!

I wondered who was coming in. Maybe it was somebody I knew. I turned around quickly . . . and saw the blue uniform of an American soldier! Before the door could close a second soldier came in behind him. They both looked dirty and dusty. All of a sudden, I didn't feel so brave. I moved slightly off to the side so a bank of the shelves hid them from my view—and me from theirs.

"Ain't much here, is there?" I heard the tall one say loudly.

"Darn near empty," the other replied. He was shorter and more heavy-set.

Silently I shifted farther over so I was even more sheltered behind the shelves.

"Here, I think we have some of the things you want!" Mr. McCann sang out as he came back into the store.

"How do you know what we might need, old man?" the first man asked.

Mr. McCann stopped dead in his tracks, too stunned to answer. His arms were filled with some of the items on my list.

"Let's have a look!" the shorter man called out as they quickly moved to his side.

I shifted again to stay out of their line of sight, crouching down behind a barrel full of axe handles.

"Hey, what do you think you're doing?" Mr. McCann demanded as the taller one grabbed him and the other took the supplies from his arms.

"Be quiet, old man, or else!"

I wanted to rush out and help him, but what could I do? There were two of them, both armed, their rifles slung over their backs.

"Looks like there's some good things here . . . things that aren't on the shelves."

"The old coot has some supplies he isn't putting out. Probably got them squirrelled away in the back. Show me where you got these from!"

"I've not got any—"

"Don't go lying to us, old man!" the shorter man yelled. Still holding Mr. McCann by the arm he started to force him toward the curtain. "You look out here while I check around back!" he called over his shoulder as he pushed through to the storeroom and dragged Mr. McCann after him.

What was he going to do to Mr. McCann? And what was going to happen to me when the other soldier found me hiding? Maybe I could get to the door and slip out.

Piiiiinnnggg!

My heart jumped up into my mouth. I couldn't see the door from where I was crouched. Was it another American soldier? Was I in more trouble? A large man ran through the door, a blur of grey, and rushed over to the soldier at the counter. The American pulled his musket off his back and started to aim at the onrushing man, who grabbed the gun before it could be levelled at him.

"Drop your weapon!" the grey-coat yelled.

His own rifle was slung across his back. He held the American's musket firm with one hand, reached out with his other hand and struck the soldier across the face. The American fell to the floor but maintained his grip on the weapon.

"Surrender and you won't be harmed!" yelled the man.

"What in God's name?"

It was the other American soldier, who must have heard the commotion! Before he could get his weapon off of his back, the man in grey, still holding the first soldier's musket in one hand, reached over and took hold of the second weapon with his other hand pulling them close! The heavy-set soldier pulled frantically to free his gun while the first, still slumped to the floor, held firm with both hands on his musket.

"Don't fire!" the taller man yelled to the other. "Your gun is aimed at me!"

"I demand that you both surrender immediately!" the grey-coat called out. His voice was remarkably calm and commanding, as if he refused to recognize that he was outnumbered.

"Are you insane?" the heavy-set man shouted.

"How dare you say such a thing!" the grey-coat declared. He struck out with a foot, kicking the man in the knee. The American groaned loudly but held tight to his weapon.

"The village is filled with soldiers. They'll come running and you'll have no choice!" screamed the soldier who'd been struck.

Of course he was right. If the grey-coat had fired his own rifle, he'd have alerted every American soldier in the village. But even if no one else arrived, he couldn't possibly hold these two off for much longer. I didn't know who this man was, but I knew he was the enemy of the Americans. That put him on our side, and he needed help.

Slowly I stood up. My knees buckled slightly. The three men were locked in struggle and nobody saw me. I slipped an axe handle out of the barrel and stole along the length of the shelf, invisible to them. I brought the handle up high above my head, leaped around the corner of the shelf and ran toward the men.

"Look out!" screamed the man on the floor, and he struggled to his feet.

The other soldier turned his head in alarm. I saw his eyes widen in shock and I hesitated for a split second before I brought the axe handle down. He turned slightly out of the way and the handle struck the side of his head, glancing down and hitting his shoulder solidly with a sickening thud. He crumpled to the floor! Blood flowed freely from his head. He was unconscious . . . or was he dead? I felt a shiver run the length of my body.

Almost immediately the grey-coat spun around and with his free hand, landed a thunderous punch to the face of the remaining American! The soldier staggered and lost his hold on the musket. The grey-coat swung the weapon and it struck the man's face. He collapsed again to the ground.

"Oh, my good Lord!" old man McCann called out. In the commotion I hadn't noticed him return from the storeroom.

"Are you loyal to the King?" the soldier demanded as he spun the gun around, pointing it at the old shopkeeper.

"To King and country," Mr. McCann sputtered. "My son is in the service of His Majesty."

"With what regiment?" the grey-coat asked.

"He's in the militia under the command of William Merritt."

"With Merritt," he said, nodding his head and lowering the gun. "What is your son's name?"

"The same as mine, Jonathan McCann."

"Jonathan McCann! I know your son! He is a good man, and it is an honour to meet his father!" The grey-coat came forward with an outstretched hand and the two men shook.

"My name is FitzGibbon. Lieutenant James FitzGibbon."

"You're FitzGibbon?" I said in amazement.

He turned to me. "I am most grateful for your actions. Without them I am not sure how long I could have held those two at bay. What is your name, son?"

"Thomas Roberts, sir," I answered nervously.

I could hardly believe it. I was standing face to face with James FitzGibbon! Everybody on the whole Niagara frontier, both Americans and Canadians, knew of him. He was the leader of the Green Tigers, a band they called "The Bully Boys," a group of British army regulars, mounted men who were feared by the Americans. Everybody had heard tales of their bold and brave deeds. They were the only soldiers loyal to the King still fighting in this part of the Niagara.

"I am most pleased to meet you, Thomas Roberts."

FitzGibbon took my hand and we shook. He was a large man, with reddish hair, wide in the shoulders, and at well over six feet he was even taller than my Pa.

"I am in your debt, sir," he said as he bowed from the waist.

I didn't know what to say . . . James FitzGibbon was in my debt!

"You saved me from an act of foolishness, Thomas. I never would have entered the store if I had realized there was more than one soldier here. I saw one horse tied to the hitching post and assumed there would be only one rider inside. I almost paid for that mistake with my freedom, possibly my—"

His speech was cut off by the sound of horses moving along the road just outside the store. FitzGibbon raced over and peeked out through the curtains.

"There are near a dozen of them . . . American cavalry. They haven't been alerted yet." He paused. "Mr. McCann, do you have rope?"

"A few coils in the back."

"Get them, please," FitzGibbon said. "I can't take these men prisoner so I'll have to restrain them."

If they had to be tied up, that meant they were still alive. Thank goodness . . . !

Mr. McCann hobbled away, but moved much more quickly than I ever remembered seeing him go before.

"Can you give me a hand, Thomas . . . do you go by Thomas?"

"Most people call me Tom, but my Pa calls me Tommy."

"And how old are you, Tommy?"

"Fourteen, sir."

He nodded his head. "I thought you were older."

"I wish I were," I told him. "Then I could be fighting beside my father."

"And where is your father?" he asked. As he spoke he took a knife from his belt and cut the ammunition bag and powder horn off one of the men.

"He's with the militia."

"With William Merritt?"

"No sir, with the Niagara brigade."

He cut away the second soldier's ammunition as well.

"Take off their shoes, Tommy."

"Their shoes?"

"Aye. There are men in the militia who have neither shoes nor shirt. I think this war is going to be decided more on proper footwear than on the accuracy of our attacks."

I looked at the shoes of the first man and then at my own bare and dusty feet. I had a pair of shoes but they were at home, safely put away. There was no point in wasting them in a walk to the village.

"Here's the rope," Mr. McCann said, handing it to FitzGibbon.

"Good!" In one powerful motion FitzGibbon grabbed the man and flipped him onto his front, pulled his hands behind him and looped the rope around his wrists.

Carefully I started to remove the shoes from the first man. I tried to be gentle . . . which suddenly struck me as strange. Just a few minutes ago I'd crowned this man with an axe handle. The side of his head was swollen and blood was still dripping from the side of his face. I could have killed him. I saw his chest rise as he took in a breath, and I took a deep breath myself in relief.

I proceeded to take the shoes from the second man. Mr. McCann was helping the Lieutenant tie up the first soldier.

"Do you live far from Queenston, Tommy?" FitzGibbon asked.

"Not far. A few miles."

"Not good," he said quietly.

Why wasn't it good? It was better than having to

trudge miles through the woods to get to the general store.

"I'll be needing some rags for gags," FitzGibbon said.

"That we surely have," Mr. McCann answered.

"I'll be needing three," the lieutenant said softly.

"Three? Why do you need three?" Mr. McCann asked.

"Begging your pardon, sir, but the third one is for you."

"Me?" Mr. McCann said, in a shocked tone that mirrored my thoughts.

"Yes. When these men are discovered they will assume that you were party to their capture, unless you too are a captive," FitzGibbon explained. "I could take you with me, but that would simply convince them that you were in league with me, and your store would surely be burned to the ground."

"They wouldn't do that, would they?" I asked.

"They would and they have," FitzGibbon said. "I've seen and heard of many things since the invasion. Houses burned, homes plundered, old men dragged from their houses and taken prisoner."

Mr. McCann shook his head slowly. "I've worked too long and hard for this store. I'll get the rags," he said, and he started to walk away.

"And Mr. McCann?"

He stopped and turned around.

"Is there anybody else in the store . . . in the back?"

Mr. McCann shook his head. "My daughter-in-law and the children have gone to spend time with her mother up by Chippawa. We thought it would be better if she were farther afield from the fort."

FitzGibbon nodded. "And you, Tommy. Did these soldiers see your face?"

I could picture the widening eyes of the one soldier before I struck him. "Yes, sir."

He nodded his head slowly. "Once these two recover their senses they will be assigned to patrols that will search the local houses and homesteads . . . for you."

"For me!" I exclaimed in shock.

"I had hoped your farm was some distance from here, but it is close enough for them to visit. And if they were to find you they might harm you, or make you a prisoner or burn down your barn and house."

"I could hide."

"You have to come with me, Tommy."

"Come with you! You want me to join the Green Tigers?" I felt a rush of fear and excitement.

He shook his head and chuckled. I felt stupid.

Of course he didn't want me to join his men. But what?

He placed a hand on my shoulder. "You've shown that you are brave, and would be a fine member of my regiment, but I must respect your parents' wishes."

I gave him a questioning look.

"If they had wanted you to be in uniform you would not still be on the farm. I just wish to have you be elsewhere for a while . . . maybe a month or so."

"I can't just go away!"

Mr. McCann, who had returned with the rags, placed a hand on my shoulder. "He makes sense, Tom. You have to go with him."

"But I'm needed on the farm, and my Ma needs to know what—"

"I'll get word to her," Mr. McCann said. "At least, once I'm untied."

"Please take great care in doing so," FitzGibbon warned. "The Americans will question you about your knowledge of the boy. If they believe you're not offering the truth it won't just be your store that is burned down."

Mr. McCann stood a little straighter. "Whether they take me prisoner or leave nothing standing but the charred remains of my store and my home, they shan't be finding anything from me." He smiled. "After all, I'm just an addled old man . . . so old he hardly knows his own name." He started to laugh, and somehow that freed us all up to chuckle along with him.

"I'll just tell 'em he was one of those beggar boys that have been wandering around since the war. That'll fool 'em."

"You have to come with me, Tommy. There's no choice. For you to stay would endanger both you—"

"I'm not afraid! I don't want to run!" I said defiantly.

"—And your family," FitzGibbon said, continuing the sentence I'd interrupted.

He was right, of course. I couldn't take a chance. I couldn't put my family in jeopardy.

"Do either of those pairs of shoes look like they might fit you?" FitzGibbon asked.

"They're both about the right size."

"Slip on a pair."

While I put on the shoes he started to tie up Mr. McCann. The shoes were a little tight in the toes, but they fit as well as my own shoes did. I tied up the laces.

"Thomas, you be careful out there," Mr. McCann said. His hands were now secured behind his back. "God save the King," he added, just before the Lieutenant slipped the gag into his mouth.

FitzGibbon gave Mr. McCann a pat on the back and then rose to his feet.

"This is the first time I've had to tie up a loyal subject of His Majesty. What I've learned is that sometimes it is better to be sly than skilled or strong. Come along now," he said, as he moved over to the window and carefully looked out. "It looks clear."

I looked too. All I could see was Mrs. Brown, a dozen buildings distant, sweeping the porch of her store. But I wondered how far away was that detachment of American cavalry who had just ridden through town.

"My horse is hitched round back. I'm going to take their guns and ammunition and go there. You must go out front, unhitch the American's horse and lead him around the side."

"Me?"

"It can't be me. It was chance enough that I came through the front door in the first place. Just move slowly, but with confidence, as though the horse actually belongs to you."

"What if somebody on the street sees me?"

"Keep your face to the horse so you can't be further identified."

"But what if it's an American soldier who sees me?"

"Keep moving to where I'll be waiting. If he follows you that far . . . he won't be following you any farther," he said, holding up the two captured guns. "Count to thirty and then go for the horse. Remember, slowly and with confidence."

FitzGibbon turned and walked to the back of the store. He stopped for an instant, reached out and placed a hand on Mr. McCann's shoulder and then disappeared through the curtain.

I had just started counting in my head when my attention was caught by the sound of a deep groan. I looked back at the three men, Mr. McCann and the two soldiers, bound and gagged by the back of the store. One of the soldiers was coming to. His eyes were still closed but he was tossing his head and moaning. I turned away and fixed my gaze back on the street.

It was still quiet outside. It was also time for me to go. I took a deep breath and opened the door.

Piiiiinnnggg! the bell called out, and I almost jumped out of my shoes . . . my stolen shoes.

The horse was tied to a hitching post at the front of

the store. It was a big grey mare. She looked to be in good shape. A dirty blue blanket peeked out beneath the saddle.

"Hello girl," I said softly. I reached out a hand and rubbed her behind the ear.

She huffed at me but accepted my hand and didn't pull away. I ran my hands down the reins to where they were tied to the post. Darn, he hadn't just looped it over, he'd tied it off. I fumbled with the knot. My hands were shaking and I suddenly felt exposed. What would they do to me if they caught me standing here in stolen shoes—shoes I'd taken from an American soldier I'd knocked on the head with an axe handle—while I was stealing his horse? What did they do to horse thieves? I stopped. I knew exactly what they did—they hanged them!

I was sweating and my heart was pounding so furiously I could feel it throughout my entire body. Between the shaking and the sweat would I ever be able to get the reins untied? Maybe I should leave the horse. I couldn't just stand there forever . . . and then the knot came free! I almost laughed out loud.

"Come on, girl," I said as I started to lead the horse away.

Slowly, keeping my head down, walking confidently as if I owned the horse. I started to round the corner of the store. This was going to work. Everything would be all right, I was sure.

"Hey there, boy! What are you doing with that horse!"

CHAPTER TWO

I FROZE IN PLACE. Slowly I swung my head around toward the voice. An American soldier, leading a horse, had come around the corner half a dozen buildings from where I stood.

"Stay where you are!" he commanded.

It wasn't hard for me to follow his order—my legs had locked in place. I didn't know if I was even capable of moving. I felt like somebody had punched me in the stomach. As I watched, a second, and a third, and then a fourth soldier appeared, all leading horses. They must have been watering their mounts at the trough beside the livery stable.

I shuddered to think what they were going to do to me . . . if they caught me. I felt a surge of energy flow through my body and I threw my foot up into the stirrup and jumped up onto the horse.

"Hey, stop!"

"*Yaaah!*" I screamed as I kicked the horse with both heels and it leaped forward. I spurred it on and we thundered around the corner of the store chased by the shouts of the soldiers behind me. I didn't want to look back but I could perfectly picture in my mind all of them hurtling into the saddles and spurring their horses forward.

I galloped around the corner and found FitzGibbon standing by his horse, the muskets slung over his shoulder.

"American soldiers!" I screamed.

"How many?"

"Four or more!" I yelled back as I reined the horse to a stop beside him.

To my utter shock, rather than leaping onto his horse he ran back the way I'd come. As he got to the corner he removed the Americans' muskets, throwing them to the ground, and levelled his own rifle. I heard the pounding of hooves and then jumped as the rifle fired and a cloud of smoke rose into the air. Before I could even react he threw the gun to the ground, grabbed a musket, levelled it and fired! Then he tossed that musket to the ground, picked up the last gun and raced toward me and his waiting horse.

Behind FitzGibbon two riderless horses emerged from the end of the alley. Where were the other two soldiers?

Suddenly FitzGibbon dropped to one knee and brought his gun up, levelling it at me! What was he doing! I crouched down, trying to hide behind the horse's neck. There was a flash of flint and an explosion as he fired!

A cry came from behind me, and in a flash I saw a horse crumple to the ground. Its rider, dressed in a blue American uniform, flew through the air, landing only yards away from me and rolling end over end. FitzGibbon rushed forward and swung his now empty gun, smashing the soldier in the face as he attempted to rise. He dropped his gun, plucked the fallen soldier's weapon from the ground and jumped up onto his horse. I could just make out the last rider, galloping hell-for-leather to round up reinforcements.

"Come on, Tommy, ride!" he screamed as he spurred his horse violently and the animal lunged forward to a path behind the store.

I dug my heels in and my horse galloped forward in pursuit of the other steed.

"Go, go, go!" I screamed. I slapped my hand against the horse's rump, coaxing it to catch up to FitzGibbon, until I was riding just behind the flank of his horse. I looked over my shoulder repeatedly. The only thing following us was the dust thrown up by our horses' hooves.

"This way!" FitzGibbon yelled.

He raced off through an opening in a rail fence surrounding an apple orchard. I knew the orchard. My brother and I had helped pick apples there the fall before. FitzGibbon charged between two rows of trees. Just before following I looked over my shoulder. Nobody was following . . . at least nobody I could see. I entered the protection of the trees and reined my horse to a stop. FitzGibbon had dismounted and was leading his mount. Some of the branches of the trees were so low that a rider couldn't get beneath them without being knocked off, especially if he was going at a full gallop.

"We have to move slowly now, Tommy."

"But we have to get away. Shouldn't we stay on the road?"

"Slow is better. Right now every American soldier who heard those shots is coming toward the town as fast as their mounts or their legs will carry them. And as we stroll through here, unseen and letting our horses rest, all around us we're being passed by those trying to—"

He stopped talking as we heard the approach of horses. It sounded like a lot of horses, moving at a fast pace. FitzGibbon motioned for me to come to him.

"Loop the reins, don't tie it off," he said as he wrapped his around a branch. I imitated his actions.

"Come," he said, and he started to go back in the direction we had just come. I moved as he did, bent over, and we both flopped down on our stomachs when we came within sight of the road.

I saw the horsemen rush by. They weren't following us, but they were rushing down the road toward the village . . . just as FitzGibbon had said. If we hadn't left the road we would have run smack into them!

I started counting after the first few riders had passed our location: eight, ten . . . eleven, twelve . . . and then three more, for a total of fifteen cavalrymen.

"Now we should be moving," FitzGibbon said.

"But what if there's another patrol still to come?"

"If there is, it'll be coming by the road. We won't be going back on that road again."

"We won't?"

He shook his head. "Never take a main road when there's a smaller road. Leave a smaller road behind when there's a country lane. Abandon a country lane when a farmer's path exists, and that same farmer's path when a forest trail crosses your path."

FitzGibbon took the reins of his horse and started to lead it, weaving through the trees.

"Are we taking the path that leads toward Chippawa?" I asked.

"Yes. You know it?"

I shrugged my shoulders. "I was born and raised here."

"That is one of our advantages around these parts. The Americans haven't got to know the area as well as we have. Of course, some of our enemies aren't from the other side of the river."

"What do you mean?"

"Men like Dr. Chapin." He said the name as though it left a foul taste in his mouth. "Have you heard of the illustrious Dr. Cyrenius Chapin?" he asked.

I shook my head.

"That would be a great disappointment to him. He's a Canadian, born and raised on this side of the border, who has thrown his lot in with the Americans. He leads a brigade of similar traitors who ride with the American invaders."

"I'd heard there were sympathizers."

"That there are. Many settlers here have roots or relatives in the States."

"We have cousins, on my Pa's side, who live outside of Lewiston, New York. My Pa said he didn't know for certain but he figured he could find himself facing family on the other side of a musket."

"I've seen that happen. It's tragic. But I'm not talking about divided loyalties but outright traitors. Chapin and his men have swooped down and taken prisoners, plundered property, and even put the torch to farms. He's done as much damage as any American invader, and it's a greater evil to do it to your own people!"

FitzGibbon stopped and turned to face me. His expression was hard, and I looked away from his fearsome gaze.

"But his time will come, and I'll be there to witness his end . . . believe me, I will."

We came to edge of the orchard and found a section of the fence where the rails had been removed and were lying on the ground.

"Did you come in this way?" I asked.

He laughed. "You're a smart lad."

We led our horses through the gap and onto the Indian path. FitzGibbon let go of the reins of his horse and went back to the fence rails. He picked up one of the rails and put it back in place. I wanted to help but I was afraid to let go of the reins of my horse in case it bolted back to its owner. FitzGibbon replaced the second and third rails, erasing the opening that marked our passage.

Then, as soon as we were both back on our horses, we made for the forest trail.

"Tell me about your family, Tommy," FitzGibbon asked as we rode.

I shrugged. "I don't know what's to tell. It's my parents, my brother Johnny, he's thirteen, my sister Sarah, she's ten, and the twins."

"A double blessing," FitzGibbon said.

"Or double trouble. They're almost four now, Elizabeth and Margaret."

"And where is your family from originally?" FitzGibbon asked.

"My grandfather came up from the States."

"Was he a Loyalist?"

"Yes, a lot of the families in these parts are. He was

loyal to the King and so he left his land and came up here after the American Revolution. My Pa said it was good Gramps didn't live to see the day those Americans would follow him across the border. He hated the Americans."

"Many of the Loyalists do, and that hatred has fuelled their fight. The Americans thought they could just march north with a few thousand men and capture the whole country. We've made them pay for each foot of soil they've captured."

I was about to answer when I looked past FitzGibbon and saw two mounted American soldiers appear around the distant curve of the path. I tried to speak, but my mouth dried up as I saw two more right behind them. I raised my hand and pointed. FitzGibbon turned and looked down the path. As we watched, more mounted soldiers appeared. Strolling along, side by side, I'd almost forgotten the reason I was here. We had to run!

FitzGibbon turned back to face me. "We're going to head for that small gap there to the right of the largest of the pine trees. When you reach the path, go to the right."

"Wouldn't it be better if you led?"

"I'll be right behind you, but first I have something to do."

"What?"

"Slowly move to the gap as I ordered. Stay shielded behind me and my mount."

Stay shielded? Why weren't we fleeing?

"Hey! Here we are! Come and get us!" FitzGibbon yelled at the top of his lungs. He had removed his hat and was waving it wildly above his head.

I practically fell off my horse in shock. What was he doing?

"Come and get me! Come on!" he yelled.

Why was he calling to them? Why weren't we running? I angled in my saddle so I could see the charging Americans . . . but they weren't charging. Instead they were fanning out across the path and levelling their guns at us! I ducked down low against my horse just a split second before I heard the loud, angry retort of guns. I heard the shots whizzing past us and through the trees.

A second volley of shot sounded and the hat FitzGibbon held was blown from his hand. FitzGibbon looked down to his hat lying on the ground, and then to me. "Get moving, Tommy!" he yelled.

I didn't need to be told again. I dug in both heels and smacked my horse on the rump for good measure. The horse balked as we neared the gap and I fought to bring it back under control. FitzGibbon and his mount surged past me into the opening and I followed.

No sooner had we found the protection of the trees than FitzGibbon slowed his horse to a trot.

"Why are we slowing down?" I demanded.

"Rough ground . . . we have to go slowly," he answered. "Besides, they won't be following us through the gap for a while."

"They won't?" I asked anxiously.

"Not likely. First they'll want to reload, and even then they'll be hesitant to follow us."

"They will?" That made no sense.

"You weren't the only one wondering what I was doing out there yelling and screaming for them to follow us. Did you think I'd taken leave of my senses?"

"No! I just . . . just . . ."

"Don't worry, lad, my actions were meant to be confusing. Those American soldiers are standing out there scratching their heads trying to figure out why I would do such a thing. A few probably think I'm crazy, but the rest might figure that I want them to follow us, that I have men waiting and I'm leading them into a trap, an ambush."

"You have men waiting?" I asked, hopefully.

"Not a one."

"But then . . . why?"

"Having them believe I have soldiers waiting is almost as good as actually having them. It's what the Americans *believe* that matters."

"Where are your men?"

"Most are camped by DeCew's Falls. That's where we're heading. A few are out in the countryside as I was, scouting the enemy's position. By nightfall there will be fifty members of the Bully Boys there."

"And the rest of your men?"

"There are no more men. That is my full detachment."

"There are only fifty Green Tigers? But there *must* be more. We're always hearing about you and your men up and down the whole Niagara frontier fighting the Americans."

"That's good to know. We want everybody to think that I have hundreds and hundreds of men under my command. That's what keeps the Americans penned in at the fort. If they ever learned just how few of us there really are, they might make more ambitious plans."

"So there isn't anybody to help us?" I asked, confused.

He shook his head. "You have to know that this is a very unequal fight we're engaged in, Tommy. We're outnumbered, out-gunned and short on everything from shoes to sugar. We have to choose our battles carefully. Through stealth and bluff, my men, supported by William Merritt's small group of militia and a band of Indians numbering no more than four hundred, have managed to keep over thirty-five hundred Americans trapped in Fort George. And when they do venture from the fort they stay hemmed close to the river or in large patrols along the major roads."

We left the woods and I fell in behind FitzGibbon as he started down the narrow trail. I continually looked over my shoulder for the Americans, but I saw nothing except the curves of the little path receding behind us. It was actually less like a path than a thin line where the grass and brush were slightly more worn down. It was hardly a path at all, although I'd walked it myself at times when I was looking for livestock that had broken through our fences or when I was out hunting with Pa. It was just hard to believe that FitzGibbon would know of this winding trail through the forest and field.

"How are your new shoes?" FitzGibbon called back over his shoulder.

"They're fine . . . they fit fine."

He started to laugh again. "I was just thinking about those two soldiers. They've probably been untied by now, along with Mr. McCann. Soon enough they'll be going barefoot and weaponless before their commanding officer. And I wonder what tale they'll be telling. Probably how they fought bravely against a band of heavily armed redcoats, but in the end were knocked unconscious and bound with rope." He paused. "And maybe other American soldiers will be hesitant to go raiding our stores, and a little bit more of our country will be safe from them . . . safe until we drive them out completely. The Americans might have struck the first blow, but in the end it will be our side that strikes the last."

I chuckled, and FitzGibbon gave me a questioning look.

"It's like my Pa always says: he's never once in his whole life struck a man . . . first."

FitzGibbon laughed. "Wise words. I would have been content to live side by side with the Americans. We didn't start this fight, but we will end it. Are you hungry, Tommy?"

"A little," I admitted. My stomach had been rumbling noisily, but that had more to do with fear than famine.

"Then we'll pick up the pace. A good supper will be awaiting us."

CHAPTER THREE

"WHO'S THAT with you?" came a voice from my left.

I jumped slightly in the saddle as I swung around to see who had spoken. I looked around anxiously in all directions but could see no one.

"His name is Thomas. Thomas Roberts!" FitzGibbon called out.

Two men dressed in the same grey uniforms as FitzGibbon came out of the woods, one on each side of the path we were travelling.

"Are all the patrols back?" FitzGibbon asked.

"You're the last. We were starting to worry that you had got yourself into some sort of trouble or mischief," one soldier answered.

"Me? What sort of trouble could I get in? Especially when I have young Tommy here to help take care of me. Thomas, meet Abraham Brown and Andrew McNeil."

The two men reached up and we shook hands.

"And Thomas here is joining our ranks?" the one called Abraham Brown asked.

"He won't be joining the Bully Boys, but he will be under our care for a few weeks," FitzGibbon answered.

"You don't usually come into camp with company, so I assume there is a story here."

"A small one . . . not particularly interesting or exciting. I'll save it until we're all sitting by the fire tonight," FitzGibbon offered.

"Looking forward to it," Andrew McNeil said. "Nothing like one of your stories."

We started off again leaving the two men behind. I looked over my shoulder and watched as, within a few strides of entering the thick underbrush, they disappeared. Something about those grey uniforms helped make them very hard to see.

"Pickets," FitzGibbon said.

"What are pickets?"

"Advance guards. We have pairs stationed around the camp at possible points of entry."

Within half a minute we'd passed out of the forest and into a field. Corn, high and ripe and ready for harvest, filled the field, and we picked our way between the tidy rows.

"This is the farm of John DeCew. It's safe here. The Americans are afraid to come this far inland and away from the river and the fort. We stay here often—but never for long."

I knew of the DeCews—I'd even met Mr. DeCew once, years before, but I doubted he'd remember me. They owned and operated a flour mill, and people from around these parts brought their grain here. Four years before I'd been to their mill with my uncle and my cousins.

Up ahead I saw a big, stone house, two storeys high. Behind it was an even larger barn, and behind that, across a large clearing, the mill sat on the bank of a creek. As we got closer I could see tents pitched in the field. A few men were visible, moving about or sitting together in groups.

We reached the barn and FitzGibbon dismounted. I climbed off my horse . . . well, at least the American soldier's horse.

"Can you bring the horses into the barn? Somebody will be in there to tend to them. Then come on over to find me and I'll get you settled in."

I took the reins of the two horses and I'd started to lead them off when I turned instead and watched FitzGibbon walk away. He was met by a group of men. They shook hands, slapped him on the back and started to talk loudly and enthusiastically. They all broke into laughter. It was just how I'd imagined it would be: a brave soldier returning from a dangerous mission, having faced death, sharing the experience with his fellow soldiers.

My stomach grumbled. I was hungry, but I'd get something to eat as soon as I got home . . . home. I wasn't going home, at least not now, and not for a while. What had I gotten myself into? All I'd wanted since the war had broken out was to be in on the adventure. Now I just wanted to go home and see my Ma and my brother and sisters and even my cousins. I suddenly felt very alone.

"Thomas!"

I looked up to see Mr. McCann . . . *young* Mr. McCann, rushing toward me!

"Thomas, what a surprise to see you! What are you doing here?"

"I was brought here—"

"Can you tell me news of my father?" he asked, interrupting me.

"I was at the store today," I answered.

"And he was fine? He was holding up okay?"

"Yes . . . he was when I left." I pictured him bound and gagged along with the two American soldiers, but I thought it best to leave that part to FitzGibbon to explain.

"Have you heard anything about *my* Pa?" I asked.

I was hoping that somebody might have heard of him, or that I might actually see him at this camp.

"Not for weeks. But don't be disappointed," Mr. McCann said, reading my expression. "There isn't much communication between our units and the others, Thomas. Merritt's men are here with FitzGibbon while the rest of the militia are stationed in Stoney Creek. That's where your father will be." He paused. "But why are *you* here?"

"Lieutenant FitzGibbon brought me. He said it wouldn't be safe after what happened in the store."

"The store? *My* store?"

I nodded. I knew this wasn't going to be easy to explain, but I couldn't wait for FitzGibbon to do it. I took a deep breath and in one long sentence I told him everything. I hesitated when I came to the part about his father having to be tied up. To my complete surprise, Mr. McCann broke into laughter.

"That's probably about the only way you could keep my father quiet! I'm just surprised it wasn't him that hit those Americans with his cane!"

"It might have been if I hadn't got there first!"

I went on to describe the escape, the chase, FitzGibbon screaming for the Americans to follow and then getting his hat shot out of his hand.

Mr. McCann shook his head and chuckled. "Lieutenant FitzGibbon has more lives than a cat and is braver than a lion! He gets into more tricky situations than you could imagine, but he always finds a way out, for himself and for any man that follows him."

"He did do that," I agreed.

"Have you eaten?" Mr. McCann asked.

"Not since before chores this morning."

"Let me take the horses and you go over and get something to eat," he said, pointing to a fire off to the side of the largest tent.

"I should really help with the—"

"Not another word," he interrupted. "Get some food and let me take care of the horses."

I hesitated. Partly because I thought I should take care of the animals myself, and partly because I was anxious about going off alone.

"Go!" he ordered, shooing me with his hands.

As Mr. McCann and the horses disappeared into the barn I slowly made my way toward the food. Over the fire, suspended on stakes, rested a large pot. Off to the side was a table that held metal plates and cups and spoons. I inhaled deeply. Whatever was cooking smelled awfully good. But that probably said more about how hungry I was than how good the food really was.

I wanted to ask somebody about eating—it just didn't seem right to help myself—but there didn't seem to be anybody to ask. Sure, there were men all around—talking, sitting and eating—but nobody seemed to be in charge. I picked up a plate and spoon and walked over to the pot. It was more than half filled with a thick, bubbly stew. It actually did look good! Not as good as my Ma's, but good enough for right now. I reached for the ladle hanging from the spit and spooned out a heaping serving. I picked a spot over by a tree and sat down by myself to eat.

* * *

BETWEEN THE men under FitzGibbon and those in William Merritt's command there were over one hundred soldiers at the DeCews'. I counted over eighty men all sitting and standing around the fire that night as FitzGibbon told the story of our adventure. People roared with laughter and yelled out comments and encouragement as he recounted the details. He was a great storyteller! At times I got so lost in the story that I had to remind myself that he was actually talking about something that had happened to me!

He concluded the tale and there was a round of boisterous applause.

"I'd like everyone to raise their cup!" FitzGibbon called above the noise.

Men called out and grumbled and talked as their cups were refilled—some with ale and some with stronger drink.

"I propose a toast!" he called out. "To a person who risked life and limb for King and country—somebody who reminds me of myself as a lad—and if not for his bravery I would not be here tonight . . . to Thomas Roberts!"

To me!

"Hear, hear!" called out many voices as the men raised their cups. A number of them then came over and shook my hand or slapped me on the back, offering congratulations or praise.

"Come on up to the house with me, Tommy," FitzGibbon said.

He ushered me through the crowd of men. They all seemed so happy and carefree, it was more like being at a barn raising than fighting a war. This was the sort of fellowship and adventure I was sure my Pa and uncle were having, and now I was part of it too. But FitzGibbon had other ideas.

"I want you to meet Mr. and Mrs. DeCew. You'll be staying with them until you hear from me again."

"Hear from you? I don't understand."

"We'll be breaking camp at sunrise. Two nights in a row at one camp is often one night too many," he explained.

"But why can't I go with you?" I asked.

"That's not possible, Tommy. I brought you here to keep you out of harm's way, not to put you in any greater danger."

"But I wouldn't be in the way. I could even help," I pleaded.

"You *will* be helping, but that help will be here. With so many men away in the militia there isn't enough help to bring in the crops."

"You mean I'll be working here . . . on this farm?" I couldn't believe it.

"That is correct. Part of the crop, ground into flour, will go back to you and your family as your wages. And part will go to other families in the area. Families that might go hungry this winter without the aid of Mr. DeCew. There's not much point in winning this war if our crops are lost and our people starve, is there? Our farms are what we'll have when it's all over. So working here will help, won't it?"

"Yes, sir . . . it will," I acknowledged. And I couldn't help thinking then of my Ma and the rest of my family, trying to work two farms with no men at home, not even me. What was I doing, dreaming of adventure, when they needed me so much? Part of me wanted to go back, but another part of me wanted to try my luck with the Bully Boys.

"You don't look happy," FitzGibbon observed.

"It's just . . . just that I . . ."

"You want to be part of our expedition."

I nodded.

"I remember how eager I was at your age. All I wanted was to leave behind my sleepy little village and find adventure. I enlisted when I was only two years older than you."

It sounded so exciting, and I wanted to be part of it all. Hadn't I proved something back there in the store?

FitzGibbon put a hand on my shoulder. "I'm certain the storekeeper has already gotten word to your mother that I've taken you away to a place of safety. And safety does not include you coming with me . . . especially with what we have planned next."

I was dying to know what he had planned, but it wasn't my place to ask.

FitzGibbon stopped at the door to the house and knocked. A woman, who was introduced to me as Mrs. DeCew, answered the door, and we were ushered into the kitchen, where Mr. DeCew joined us. He was older—and smaller—than I remembered. They were nice people and they made me feel comfortable and welcome. Mrs. DeCew then took me upstairs and showed me where I'd be sleeping. It was a big, spacious room—much bigger than the one I shared with my brother. I wondered if I'd be able to sleep without him pulling off the blankets and kicking me.

When we returned to the kitchen, FitzGibbon was sitting at the table with Mr. DeCew and another man. Spread out in front of them was a large piece of paper, a roughly drawn map. They were talking very loudly and seemed to be in the middle of an argument. Who was this man that he would argue with FitzGibbon?

FitzGibbon looked up. "Tommy, come, I want you to meet somebody. This is William Merritt, the leader of this militia division."

"I'm pleased to meet you," I said as we shook hands.

He didn't look much older than me! I couldn't believe that anybody that young could be in charge.

I must have been staring because FitzGibbon said, with a smile, "Yes, he is very young," and I felt myself blush.

All three men laughed.

"I get that all the time," Mr. Merritt said. "I'm twenty."

Embarrassed, I dropped my gaze to the crude, sketched-out map on the table. It showed the Niagara River and the creeks leading into it, Fort George, Queenston, and on the American side, Fort Niagara and Lewiston. Just north of Lewistown was a red X.

"Thank goodness you're not an American spy or you'd know our plans," FitzGibbon said, pointing to the map. "X marks the spot."

"I didn't mean to spy, honestly!" I said, alarmed.

"It's all right, Thomas." FitzGibbon chuckled. "I was just having fun with you."

"Are you really going to invade the States?" I asked in amazement.

"Not invade," FitzGibbon explained. "But we are going to make a trip over to the American side to liberate some supplies. There is a storage depot that supplies the American army at Fort George. If we take away their food and supplies we could cripple them. After all, an army moves on its stomach. This could be a decisive strike against the enemy!"

"Or against us," Merritt said.

"Come now, William, I'm sure it will succeed . . . and you know how much I respect you." He paused. "I must admit, your concerns have raised doubts for me."

"It's just too risky, James."

"But worth the risk if it works! Not only will it give us needed supplies and deprive them of resources, but it will strike fear into their hearts!"

"I know all the arguments, James, and I agree with them. An attack across the river would even force them to withdraw some of their soldiers back onto American soil."

"Exactly my point!" FitzGibbon said, pounding his fist on the table. He was certainly convincing.

"If only we were operating on our ground. Our

success so far has come from knowing the trails and coun-tryside better than the Americans," Merritt added.

"Some of your men must be familiar with the area," FitzGibbon suggested.

"Familiar, yes . . . familiar in the same manner that the Americans are familiar with our side of the river, and you can see how little that has helped them."

"I know the area," I said quietly.

Both men stopped talking and looked at me.

"Remember when I said I had relatives on the American side of the river?" I asked.

FitzGibbon nodded.

"Four summers ago, when my Ma was expecting the twins, she was having a rough time. My brother and sister and I were still too young to be much help, so we spent the entire summer with our relatives. Their farm is right there," I said, placing a finger just down from the red X. "My cousin and I used to ride his horses all through the area, we fished on the river . . . I even know the trails up the cliffs."

FitzGibbon reached out and pushed the map toward me. "Here," he said, handing me a piece of charcoal. "Sketch what you have just described."

"I'm not much at drawing," I said, taking the charcoal.

"We're not looking for a work of art. Any details you can add would be invaluable to us."

I put the tip against the paper. First I added some details to the Canadian side of the river—a couple of back roads and the trail that FitzGibbon and I had followed. Next I found the spot where we always crossed the river. I traced a line with my finger across the river, but diagonally, the way our boat always got pushed downstream during a crossing.

"This is where we usually land," I said. "There's a flat spot and easy access up the cliff."

"And you think that spot would be a better landing than here?" FitzGibbon asked, pointing to another spot upstream.

"I don't know . . . we always put in here . . . and I figure my father did that because it was the best spot," I answered.

"And how would you get from that spot to the supply depot up here?" FitzGibbon asked.

I put the charcoal to the paper again. "There's a farmer's lane at the top that leads this way . . . I mean this way," I said. Although I could picture it in my mind, I couldn't remember where the lane started. "I'm just not sure, but I could find my way if I was there, for sure. And once you're on that trail it will lead you right to the place you've marked on the map. Of that I'm sure," I said.

"Having a guide who knows the area changes everything," Merritt said.

Did he mean me? I looked at FitzGibbon. He didn't look happy about the suggestion.

"It would put us on a level footing with the Americans who know the area," the younger man said, trying to convince FitzGibbon. "Would you be willing to come along with us, Tommy?"

"That is not a question that should be asked," FitzGibbon said.

"I'm sorry, James," Merritt said. "It's just that it could make such a difference . . . the difference between life and death."

"I didn't bring Tommy away from his family to place him in greater danger."

"We can minimize the danger. He could lead the way to the trail at the top and then return to the boats to wait with the guards."

"Tommy, would you please excuse us?" FitzGibbon said. "William . . ." He motioned for Merrit to follow as he walked out of the kitchen. A door swung shut behind them.

"For my part, I hope they leave you here," Mr. DeCew said. "We could certainly use the help around the farm and mill. But if it were up to you, Tommy, what would you choose?"

I did want to be part of their adventure, and I certainly didn't want to work at somebody else's farm, but still . . . maybe it would be better to remain.

Before I could answer the door opened and FitzGibbon and Merritt reappeared.

"Tommy, do you want to go for a boat ride?" FitzGibbon asked.

CHAPTER FOUR

SILENTLY THE men dipped oars into the water. There wasn't a sound except the waves washing against the sides of the boat. Both sides of the river were pitch black. The only light at all was from the moon and stars, which were peeking through swirling clouds of mist that blanketed the water.

It was cool, but not cool enough to explain why I was shivering. I'd had more than second thoughts about agreeing to come along. Staying at the DeCews' farm wouldn't have been nearly as exciting but it certainly would have been safer. And warmer.

The Lieutenant and I were in the lead boat, the biggest vessel, along with twenty others. Around us, in a dozen other boats of different sizes and shapes, were the other eighty who made up FitzGibbon's and Merritt's detachments. We didn't need this many vessels to transport the men, but we'd use them to bring back the supplies they were hoping to capture.

The Lieutenant said I could come as far as the start of the trail and then, at that point, he'd sent me back with a rear guard to stand over the boats.

"Ever travel the river at night?" FitzGibbon asked.

"Never," I admitted. "It seems quiet . . . peaceful."

"And dark. If the Americans on either side of the river saw us out here we'd have a welcoming party waiting for us no matter where we put in."

"They can't see us now, right?" My doubts were suddenly overwhelming my confidence.

"Not a chance. Can you even see the other boats?" he asked.

I looked back and strained my eyes. I could only barely make out the outlines of the next two or three boats behind us, and the rest were invisible. I guess he was right. Between the dark and the mist we were safe from prying eyes.

"Are we coming in at the right place?" FitzGibbon asked of the soldier manning the rudder.

"The current is strong. It's a struggle to stay on course, but I'm doing my best," he answered. "The other boats are smaller and might be pushed farther down river than us."

"Not good. We might not have enough time to regroup before heading inland and then getting back to the Canadian side before the sun comes up. Put your backs into it lads and let's make land."

We were still too far offshore to make out anything except the darkened outline of the cliffs rising up on the other side.

Free to think, I couldn't keep my mind off what we were doing. I hadn't stopped thinking about it since FitzGibbon had agreed to let me come along. We'd left the DeCew farm the next morning and camped closer to the river so we could leave the following night. I felt scared—not that something was going to happen to me, but about not being able to find the trail. It had been four years since that summer, and trails can disappear quickly if they're not used. Besides, I'd only been out on the trails during the day, and we'd be travelling by night. It would be awful if they trusted me to lead them and I couldn't.

They would all think I had been full of bluster. Like my Pa always said, an empty barrel makes the loudest sound. The lump in my stomach got bigger.

"Feeling nervous?" FitzGibbon asked me.

"Some."

"It's not too late to change your mind. You can remain with the boats."

"You need me to find the trail."

"We'll find the trail with or without you," he said.

"But . . ." It suddenly dawned on me. "You don't want me to be here, do you?"

He didn't say anything for a moment.

"It's true. I'd rather you had stayed at the DeCew farm," he said then. "But you know the terrain, and that knowledge might save the lives of my men and those of William Merritt."

Before I could respond the boat ran against something and I was rocked forward. I stood up and saw that we'd hit rocks just off the shore. Some of the men pulled their oars out of the water and used them as poles to push off the rocks. Then one man, holding a rope, jumped into the waist-deep water and waded to shore. Two others jumped in after him, followed by FitzGibbon. The boat was pushed and pulled forward then until it was safely beached. Wordlessly, the rest of the men got out of the boat. Each held his gun, powder and shot high above his head. If water got to any of those, then the muskets would be useless.

I climbed out and into the water. A shiver went up my spine that had more to do with fear than the coldness of the water. I couldn't help but think of FitzGibbon's offer. Maybe I should stay by the boats. Then I thought about all the other times I'd crossed this river before. Always during the day, and always with my Pa at my side. I wondered where he was now. All I knew for sure was that wherever he was, he was doing his part to defeat the Americans, and I had to do my part too. I'd lead them to the trails.

"Do you know where we are, Tommy?" FitzGibbon asked.

"I think so. We came in a bit father down river than I thought we should. We'll have to backtrack along the shore . . . maybe half a mile."

"McNab, Jamison and Johnson are to stay with the boat. Alexander, I want you to take a party of two and go downstream to locate the other boats. Lead them back this way. We'll be at the top of the heights waiting," FitzGibbon said.

I looked out over the water and didn't see anything. I remembered what I'd heard about the current being strong.

"All others come with me."

I took to FitzGibbon's side and together we started to lead.

During the time it took us to cross the river the moon had risen higher in the sky. It threw off a little more light, which allowed me to recognized our location. A flat strip of land was wedged between the water and the cliff. There were very few trees or even bushes. That made the trip easy; of course, it also meant no cover to hide behind. I could picture unseen eyes peering down at us as we moved. I was pleased, at least, that the mist was spilling over the river and onto the flats.

"The path isn't far from here," I said after we'd walked for awhile. "It branches off the road that runs along the top."

"Good. Tommy, I want you to head back to the—"

"I thought I was going as far as the path?"

FitzGibbon paused. In the dark I couldn't read his expression.

"Last two in line stay here and direct the coming parties to follow us," FitzGibbon directed. "Follow behind Tommy and me."

My smile was lost in the darkness.

We moved up the trail and the rest of the line followed behind. I looked back over my shoulder as I started up the incline. What had begun as a force one hundred strong was now down to me, FitzGibbon and eleven men—thirteen of us. I wasn't superstitious but somehow that number didn't seem like a good omen.

The trail up the cliff was steep and I found myself labouring for breath before we'd reached the crest. I stopped at the top. The mist, which had been thinning out as we moved up, was now almost completely gone. FitzGibbon motioned for the men to fan out across the top of the cliff.

"It's important to always claim the highest ground. From this point, we'll be able to cover our retreat across the flats to the boats. We'll have to be prepared in case there is pursuit. Can you direct us from here?"

"The road starts at the far end of this meadow," I said. "And the path is close from there."

"Good. I'm going to send you back down to wait by the boats."

"But I thought—"

"Come, Tommy, it was agreed that you weren't coming all the way on this trip. I have to send you back."

"I know," I agreed. "It's just . . ."

"Just what?" FitzGibbon asked.

"I know exactly where we are, and I know the path is just up ahead somewhere, but it's been four years since I was here and I want to make sure I don't steer you in the wrong direction. Maybe things have changed . . . like I don't remember there being a barn up here."

"A barn? I don't see anything."

"Over there at the edge of the meadow. Can't you see its outline?"

"I can see something, but it doesn't look like a barn," he answered.

The silence of the night was broken by the piercing sound of a bugle. I jumped at the sound, which continued as torches appeared around the building. In the light I could see soldiers, lots of soldiers, flowing out of a door and into the meadow. My heart rose up into my throat.

"Militia from the looks of them," FitzGibbon said. His voice was calm, the complete opposite of what I felt.

"Do they see us?" I asked anxiously.

"They wouldn't have blown assembly if they hadn't. There must have been pickets on the top of the hill who rushed back to report when they saw us coming. Tommy, I need you to go down the trail and direct the men up to us. I need to assemble my men before the enemy attacks."

I was confused. "You already left somebody down below to send men up the trail,"

"They might not know they have to hurry. I need speed. Speed from both you and them! Go! Do as you've been ordered!"

I started away.

"And Tommy, tell them to make noise when they return."

"Noise?" I asked.

"Lots of noise. Tell them to drag their feet and raise their voices. I need each man to sound like ten. Go!"

I stumbled down the trail. I had to hurry, and I guess it didn't matter how much noise I made. Surely by now some of the other boats had put in and the men had found their way to the foot of the cliff. I doubled my pace. My feet slid on some gravel and I slipped, almost falling over, regaining my balance only at the last second. Then I stumbled again and fell head first, skidding to a stop, a small hail of stones continuing down the slope before me. I tried to get back to my feet but tumbled forward again. This wasn't working. I'd have to slow down to go faster. My eyes were well adjusted to the night, but there still wasn't enough light to see clearly.

I got to my feet slowly and started down the slope again. I didn't know what was going on above my head, but it was best I didn't think about it. The trail flattened out and I picked up speed. Within seconds I saw the first two men.

"Americans! There's Americans at the top of the cliff!" I called out as I skidded to a stop in front of them.

"How many?" one of them demanded.

"I don't know . . . lots I think . . . the Lieutenant sent me to get more men, he needs more soldiers up top as soon as possible! Where is everybody?"

I'd no sooner asked the question than we heard the sound of men making their way along the river.

"We'd better call them over," I said.

I started to walk toward the noise when one of the men grabbed me from behind and pulled me down.

"What are you doing?" I demanded as I struggled to free myself. "We've got to let them know we're—"

A hand was pressed tightly against my mouth, cutting off my sentence.

"Shhhhh!" he hissed at me "Maybe we don't want them to know we're here."

The hand over my mouth was released.

"But why?" I whispered.

"Do you have the eyes of an owl?" he asked.

"Of course not."

"Then how do you know those aren't American soldiers? Stay here and stay silent," one of the soldiers said.

The two men rose and started moving toward the sounds coming down the river. I braced myself for gunshots I hoped wouldn't come. Was it possible we were trapped between two columns of Americans? Seconds passed . . . seconds that seemed like hours. The sounds got louder. Whoever they were, they were moving closer. At least I wouldn't have to wait much longer . . . the waiting was the hardest part.

"Tommy!" somebody called out.

I'd never been so relieved to hear my name. I could make out dark figures coming out of the mist. They materialized into the familiar faces of William Merritt and Mr. McCann, moving at double time. Behind them the mist released a double row of soldiers. Before the first two reached me I had counted ten men.

"Tommy, where do we go?" demanded Merritt.

"It's over that way and then . . ." I could tell them, but

I knew it would be faster if I led them. So what if FitzGibbon had ordered me to come down here? I did retreat to the flats, just as he'd ordered. He hadn't said anything about not coming back.

"Follow me," I called out, and I started back toward the trail up the cliff.

Hitting the slope I slowed my pace. Remembering what FitzGibbon had said about making noise I began to drag my feet against the rock and gravel.

"The Lieutenant wanted people to come back noisy," I called over my shoulder. "He wants them to think—"

"That we're a larger force than we are," Merritt said, completing my sentence. "Do you know how many Americans there are?" he asked.

"I don't know. They were still coming out of the building when I left. I think there are a lot of them."

"Maybe not. We haven't heard any gunfire. If I was commanding a large force I would have already closed in on the enemy before he gained strength," Merritt said.

FitzGibbon was waiting at the very top of the trail. It were hard to see clearly in the dark but I think he scowled when he saw that I'd returned. The scowl was replaced with a smile when he recognized William Merritt.

"How many are with you?" FitzGibbon asked.

"Sixteen men."

I was hoping he was going to say more than that.

"I've left four soldiers to direct the remainder of the men to our position."

"You certainly sounded like a force of hundreds," FitzGibbon replied. "Have your men fan out, half in each direction, under cover of the trees and brush that run along the top of the cliff. When they've taken positions I want them to advance a few paces and strike a kneeling position, ready to shoot, but so they don't obstruct the fire of the men in the second and third rows."

"Second and third rows?" Merritt demanded. "What second and third rows?"

"The ones I'm hoping the Americans will see in their imaginations."

Merritt turned to McCann. "Have the men follow the directions of the Lieutenant."

"Yes, sir!" he answered, and he retreated to give the orders.

"What is the strength of the enemy, James?" Merritt asked.

"It's a militia force. I haven't seen any blue uniforms or cannon. It numbers between two and three hundred."

"Two and three hundred! Even if our entire force

gathered here in time we would still be outnumbered by a margin of close to three to one! Should we not be retreating?"

"Retreat is not advisable. Retreat would cost us our only two advantages—the high ground and deception," FitzGibbon said calmly. "Tell me, William, what would you do if you were in command of three hundred men facing an enemy numbering forty?"

"Why, I'd press forward with an attack, losing not a second."

"As would I. So why haven't they attacked? Maybe their officer is inexperienced or timid. Maybe he is experienced but realizes that his men do not have the heart for a fight. I would also say with some certainty that the mist and darkness below and dim light and cover here make it near impossible for him to accurately know the size of our force. So he must read our actions. If we retreat, it will be because we are of inferior numbers, and he will be able to spur his forces on to pursue us. Nothing promotes bravery as much as seeing your enemy flee. But if we are to stand our ground, he will have to assume that we are in possession of a force at least as great as that under his command. Do you see the interesting challenge before us, William?"

"I do, but we can't simply remain here indefinitely. At first light he'll be able to see our numbers clearly. We must move back down to the river before then."

"I agree, we must move . . . forward."

"You want us to attack!"

Merritt's voice reflected my shock. Even FitzGibbon couldn't think he could win this battle!

"I did not say attack. I said forward. And that I will be doing alone. I wish to meet the American commander under a flag of truce and test my beliefs about their resolve to do battle. William, you are in command of both units in my absence."

He placed his rifle and pack on the ground. Then he picked up a long stick that had a piece of white cloth attached at the end. Obviously this had been his intention for a while and he had prepared for it.

"Well Tommy, are you ready to go?"

He was sending me away, back to the boats. "Yes, sir."

"You don't seem very excited."

"I thought maybe I could stay here to see what was going to happen," I said.

"Believe me. You will see things very closely. You are coming with me."

"I am?" I asked in shock.

"Come when I call," was his answer.

"Yes, sir."

FitzGibbon began walking toward the American position, waving the white flag of truce above his head. At the far side of the meadow I could just make out the outline of the ranks of American soldiers, strung out in a thin line the width of the meadow. And while I was certain we were still out of musket range, I knew we wouldn't be for long.

"Attention!" FitzGibbon bellowed, and I jumped slightly. "I come under a flag of truce!" he yelled, and his voice echoed back at us through the night air.

Silence.

"Will you accept my truce!" he called again.

By now, even the crickets had stopped chirping.

"Come forward," called out a voice at last. "You are allowed to approach under the flag of truce."

"We are proceeding!" FitzGibbon yelled back. He motioned for me to come to his side.

"No matter what I say, you must nod your head in agreement. Now come, and don't be afraid. We are under truce. The Americans might be our enemies, but they are people of integrity and will honour the truce as surely as we would."

FitzGibbon handed me the flag. He started forward and I fell into step beside him. He was setting a quick pace, showing no fear, and I struggled to match his strides.

"I want to view their positions, see the faces of the men on the line, and let them hear my words," he said, and he started to move with even greater urgency.

Soon I could almost make out the faces of the men who were standing before us. The line curved out of view in both directions. We moved so close that I could hear a murmur of conversation and coughing among the ranks. FitzGibbon suddenly stopped, and I almost bumped into him.

"I am a lieutenant, upon the orders of Colonel Bisshopp. I await your commander!" he called out.

He leaned over to me and spoke softly. "I want them to think there is a full colonel waiting in the unseen darkness. A colonel might mean a force of five hundred men."

Two men pushed through the American ranks. One was a soldier carrying a flag of truce similar to the one that I held, and the uniform of the second included a distinctive black felt hat, which identified him as an officer. They stopped in front of us.

"At your service, sir!" FitzGibbon said, saluting the enemy officer.

The officer saluted back. "I am Major Hall, commander of the American militia detachment. We have honoured your truce, Lieutenant. What do you wish to discuss?"

"My commanding officer has asked me to make an offer to yourself and to the men in your charge."

"And what is that offer?"

"Amongst our command are two regiments of militia who have been recruited from directly across the river, among them this young lad, who is my bugler," he said, motioning to me.

A bugler? I'd never even held a bugle before, but I knew that large companies often had buglers . . . this was more of the deception to convince them that we were a large force of men.

"The militia commander has stated that his men will follow orders, but that they do not wish to fire upon men who are their neighbours, some of whom are friends or even family," FitzGibbon continued. The Lieutenant cleared his throat noisily. "I see you are all militia," he announced in a loud voice.

Why was he talking so loudly? The Major was no more than a few feet in front of us.

"And we do not wish to be killing the husbands, fathers and brothers of our neighbours across the river!" FitzGibbon finished loudly.

I noticed that all the talking and coughing and shifting of feet among the American lines had stopped. They were listening to him. Everybody who could hear was hanging on his every word.

"We make a promise that no home will be entered nor homestead harmed! You shall all be allowed to retire to your homes!" he practically yelled.

"That is a most generous offer you are making, Lieutenant, and if you would allow me time to consider such an offer I would . . ." Major Hall stopped talking as we all heard a rumbling and shuffling behind him. He turned toward his lines.

Before our eyes the soldiers on the line closest to us were drifting away. At first it was just a few men, and then a few more, and then the line started to crumble in both directions into the darkness. Rather than simply slowly backing away, some men then turned and began running at a full trot.

"Stop your men!" FitzGibbon called out. "This is quite irregular to retire in such a manner while negotiating under a flag of truce!"

"I know it, sir!" Major Hall exclaimed.

"I must insist that you have them reassemble and then retreat in an orderly and more military manner. Please have them return to their ranks immediately!" FitzGibbon demanded.

"I do not possess the power to stop them!" Major Hall practically yelled out.

The line was now almost completely gone.

"But I do have the power to accept your offer. Please advise your commanding officer that I have agreed to the terms of the truce and my men are in the process of retiring to their homes." He raised his hand and saluted FitzGibbon.

FitzGibbon returned the salute. "A most wise decision, sir!"

Major Hall and his aide turned and retreated from the field. No sooner had the darkness swallowed them up than FitzGibbon burst into laughter—a laughter that I was sure could be heard by both the retreating Major and our own ranks across the meadow.

CHAPTER FIVE

"YOU DID IT, James!" William Merritt roared as he pumped FitzGibbon's hand.

"I don't think they'll stop running until each man is safely at home, hiding beneath his bed or behind his wife's petticoats," FitzGibbon replied. "And our men?"

"We have eighty-four positioned along the top of the cliff. The remainder are below, guarding the boats. Some of the boats put into shore much farther downstream, but all have now been gathered together at the place where your vessel came to shore."

"Excellent, excellent!"

"Should I order retreat?" Merritt offered. He paused and a smile came to his lips. "Or shall we . . ."

FitzGibbon nodded. "I would imagine that the entire defence for this whole sector was housed in those barracks. And now there isn't an American between here and the supply depot. I believe we should continue with our original plan. We'll leave a party of ten men to hold the entrance to the trail and proceed with the remainder of our company."

Merritt slapped FitzGibbon on the back and then left to gather the men into formation.

"Well, Tommy, I'll now offer you a choice," FitzGibbon said. "You may retire to the boats or come with us to the supply depot. Which shall it be?"

"I was thinking I've come this far, so maybe I should go the rest of the way," I answered. I didn't want to be deprived of the adventure that they were going to have just so I could stand by the river watching some old boats. Besides, with all the Americans in flight, what danger would there be?

"Good lad!"

Within minutes the men had assembled into four squads of roughly eighteen men. Two of the groups were militia attached to Merritt while the other two were members of the Bully Boys. The militia split off to either side, flanking the two squads of FitzGibbon's men, who fell in behind the Lieutenant and myself. Once again I was going to show them the way.

As we passed by the deserted militia barracks I couldn't help but think of what would have happened if they hadn't accepted FitzGibbon's pardon to return to their homes. It wouldn't have been a simple walk across the field but an impossible dash through a thicket of musket fire.

We cleared the field and were funnelled down the narrow road through thick forest cover. Merritt's squads were forced off our flanks and fell back to the rear. This trail led south toward Lewiston. I could still taste the dust in the air, thrown up by the retreating Americans. We needed to follow it only as far as the trail cutting back downstream toward the supply depot. I knew the trail—I'd ridden or walked on it dozens of times—but I was having trouble locating the entrance in the dark.

"Do you need us to slow the pace?" FitzGibbon asked. "I know this is a task made more difficult by the dark of night."

"No it's fine . . . or maybe just a little," I admitted.

I kept my eyes trained to one side. I remembered the entrance was in the middle of a stand of birch trees, with one especially tall tree marking the very beginning. But in the dark, the trees all had a sameness to them, and the tips of the tallest were lost in the night sky.

It would be awful if I couldn't find the path. I'd have let everybody down and there would be nothing left but to head back across the river . . . back over to Canada.

I thought about my little piece of Canada: our cabin and the barn, the fields and forest and the stream running through . . . the stream! That was right, there was also a stream just past the entrance to the path, and we'd just crossed over a stream.

"We need to go back," I said. "I think we've missed it."

FitzGibbon raised his hand and the column came to a stop. He turned to the men directly behind him. "First four men, proceed one hundred yards down the way and take up position."

They followed his directions.

"All others, rest and water. And I want those men with trinkets to secure them so you aren't jingling like a sled ride."

The column split in two as men left the road, removed their packs and sat down, resting their backs against the bordering trees.

"Did you hear that noise as we moved?" FitzGibbon asked.

"I heard something, like metal rattling."

"Good-luck charms, lockets, all manner of trinkets. Everybody has a tale about somebody whose life was saved when he was shot at and the musket ball was stopped by a metal trinket he was wearing."

"That's incredible!"

"Incredible, but in truth all those trinkets have cost more lives than they'll ever save. Silence is more important than luck when attacking at night. How far back do you think the path is?" FitzGibbon asked.

"Not far. I think it's just ahead of the stream we crossed."

"Think or know?"

"Think," I reluctantly admitted.

"Let's go back then and try to locate it."

I moved as quickly as I could without looking desperate. I didn't want everybody to know I'd made a mistake until they also knew I'd successfully found the right way. Most of the men had taken out their canteens, I could heard some talking, and a few had grabbed a bite from their rations. It was too dark to make out their faces clearly but I knew all eyes were trained on me as I moved past. The column was long. The sixty men were in pairs but they were well spread out.

No sooner had I passed the last man than I came to the stream. Anxiously I searched the bush, looking for the opening or the stand of birch trees. Everything always looked so different in the dark. Then, practically right in front of me, I spied the opening. The way the trail angled into the road made it hard to see in the direction we'd been moving but almost impossible to miss coming back this way. My feet moved even faster on the way back to tell the Lieutenant that I'd found it!

*   *   *

SILENTLY OUR force spread out to surround the blockhouse where the supplies were kept. It was a large, wooden structure surrounded by a sizeable log wall, and it reminded me of a small fort. There was a gate at the front, closed now, slots in the walls from which muskets could be fired or the forest observed, and small covered areas on the roof that could conceal guards. There was no telling how many men were on guard or inside.

Everybody was under orders to remain hidden in the forest unseen and unheard by those who might be watching and listening. I was now glad that FitzGibbon had ordered the men to secure their good-luck charms. The Lieutenant thought he might have enough men to launch an attack, coming at it from three sides, and we were dispersed for just such an offensive. But first he wanted to try something different. He was going to try to trick his way through the gate. If anybody could do it, it was FitzGibbon.

I lay in the bushes, hiding behind tree and cover, and looked down the roadway that connected Fort Niagara and Lewiston. Our route had crossed the road half a mile back, and at that point FitzGibbon, William Merritt and three other men had left us while we proceeded to our spots.

Just before we'd reached our positions, still safely out of sight and sound of the blockhouse, the company had come to a stop. All at once those members of the regular army, those under the command of FitzGibbon, removed their grey jackets and replaced them with the scarlet uniform of the British Army, which they always carried in their packs. At first I didn't understand why they were doing this—putting on uniforms that would draw attention to them. It was explained to me that if they had to storm the blockhouse the Americans would be more frightened to see the red of regular British soldiers and more likely to surrender without a fight. Besides, as I soon saw in the pitch black of the forest, they were not much more visible than the grey.

When the Lieutenant left he had put me in the charge of Mr. McCann. Though my old neighbour treated me more like the young boy I used to be than the young man I'd become, I had to admit that he made me feel safe. I trusted Mr. McCann. My Pa always spoke highly of him.

"How many soldiers do you think are inside?" I asked him in a hushed tone.

"Can't be certain. It's a large building. Could be fifty, although likely no more than two dozen," he whispered into my ear. "But you can be certain they'll be blue-coats, regular army and not militiamen."

I heard the approach of feet along the road and soon I could make out the first faint outlines of five men. I thought it must be FitzGibbon and the rest, but in the darkness I couldn't be completely certain.

"I wish it wasn't both FitzGibbon and Merritt out there," Mr. McCann whispered in my ear. "I shudder to think what would happen to the whole of the Niagara region if something were to happen to those two."

"They'll be fine," I whispered back. I couldn't even imagine anything befalling FitzGibbon.

"I'm sure you're right. No two men are better for the job. But if you dance with danger often enough . . ."

He let the sentence trail off as the men came to a stop thirty paces from the gate of the blockhouse.

"Hello! We are friends!" cried out a voice. It was William Merritt's.

"Identify yourselves!" came the answer from the blockhouse.

"We are militia from the Lewiston detachment and are answering to the orders of Major Hall!"

"And what might those orders be?" called back the voice.

"I'm not party to the Major's secrets!" Merritt answered back.

I saw a flash of white—it looked like an envelope— held high above his head.

"I have sealed orders. But I think they might have something to do with the British invasion and attack on Fort Schlosser!"

Mr. McCann leaned close to my ear. "Brilliant. Give them a little tidbit that they can't help but want to know about. And to announce a British invasion like that! No one would suspect a redcoat to be giving such news!"

"Come forward and be identified!" came the answer from the blockhouse.

Maybe this was going to work, and they'd talk their way through the gate.

At the corner of the wall a torch was struck and the bright semicircle of light exposed three soldiers, one holding the torch and two standing off to the side holding muskets. Suddenly the torch was tossed through the air, spinning end over end to land on the ground a dozen paces in front of the gate.

"Come forward into the light!" called out the voice.

"You stay right here, no matter what happens!" Mr. McCann whispered firmly.

"No matter what happens? Isn't it working?" I asked.

"I don't know, but I don't like them having to come forward like that. Once they're in the halo of the light they'll be a target for every musket on the wall, and they themselves won't be able to see a thing in the darkness. You're to stay here—promise me."

"I promise."

The five men entered the pool of light. They spread out so that all could be seen. Their weapons were on their backs.

"Are you men with the militia of Major Hall?" asked the voice.

"No, we were sent from Fort Schlosser with word to Major Hall to bring his militia to that area. It was he who asked us to bring this message farther to this depot before returning to our posts," Merritt explained.

"And why didn't he send his own men?" asked the voice. "They're mostly faces we are familiar with."

"He wanted his squads to go as a whole. Besides he felt after our march to Lewiston we weren't good for much except delivering messages!"

There was a long pause. Mr. McCann was right, this wasn't going well. Inside the walls they were deciding what to do next while the five men stood outside, completely exposed in the light.

"Keep your word, remain here," Mr. McCann whispered. He drew himself up from his belly and got to his knees. The men within my sight had done the same. They were getting ready to charge the walls of the blockhouse.

"Begging your pardon, sir!" cried out a voice— FitzGibbon's! "We're tired and hungry we is, and we was hoping for a place to lay down our heads and a nip to drink, but if you're fearful we can leave the orders here and go our way!"

There was no answer.

"We'll just leave the orders and be gone!" Merritt said. He bent down and went to place the envelope on the grass.

"That won't be necessary!" called out the voice from the blockhouse. "Come forward and be admitted!"

The five men proceeded out of the bright light and toward the gate. I let out a deep sigh. They had bluffed their way into the blockhouse. Once they were admitted, they'd block the gate and our men would rush in, over-whelming the soldiers within. They'd done it—just as I knew they—

The darkness was split by the explosion of a gunshot, and then a second, and third, and a volley of muskets! In shock I looked first at Mr. McCann and then at the gate to the blockhouse. More shots rang out and a man fell to the ground!

CHAPTER SIX

"FOR KING and Country!" Mr. McCann shouted.

He rose to his feet, along with men on all sides, and charged out of the forest and into the clearing surrounding the blockhouse. Each man screamed as he ran forward, and their roar was punctuated by the explosion of musket fire. The smell and smoke of the shot filled the air.

The rush of excitement caused me to leap to my feet

as well, and I had to fight the urge to run forward with the men. Instead I followed to the edge, to the very last tree, and stopped—I needed to see, but I also needed to keep my word. Spread out before me, at the front and both sides of the blockhouse that I could see, men had closed the open ground from the meadow and were at the walls. The front gate was still open and I could make out redcoats and militia streaming through the gap and into the fortification. I wished I could be there, inside the gate, watching, seeing, knowing all that was happening instead of under cover in the trees, hiding from the musket fire. Then the sound of the guns suddenly stopped. And the cries of the men ceased as well, leaving nothing but a complete and eerie silence. The smoke clung in the air. The smell was bitter and strong in my nose and mouth.

I ventured out of the forest and into the clearing. The torch was still lying on the ground by the gate. Although its flame had died down, its light still illuminated the entrance and reached almost to where I stood. Half a dozen of our soldiers were standing at the gate, indicating that whatever had happened was done and that our side had been victorious. No one would object if I joined them now.

As I approached, the six men at the gate split off into two groups. Three went up the road toward Lewiston while the others went down the road in the direction of Fort Niagara.

Immediately I knew what was being done: pickets were being sent out to guard the approaches to the blockhouse, to warn of approaching soldiers. There was no telling how far afield the sounds of the battle had travelled.

I braced myself and then peeked through the gate. Other torches had been lit and I could clearly see the ground between the wall and the blockhouse. There were American soldiers, at least twenty, standing in the open, their arms in the air, with a ring of militia and redcoats standing guard, muskets at the ready. There were a few blue-coats lying on the ground beside the others— wounded, I guessed.

I'd seen one of our men go down at the gate. Was it FitzGibbon, or Merritt, or one of the others? I had to find out.

I stepped in through the gate and stumbled. I looked back. I'd tripped over the legs of a man lying on the ground.

"I'm sorry," I stammered.

"Save your breath, he won't be hearing you."

I turned around to face the voice. It was one of our men, Jennings. I didn't understand what he meant until

I looked closer at the fallen soldier. He wore a blue American uniform. The front was smeared with the red of blood.

"Is he . . . ?"

"He'd better be dead," the soldier offered.

I stepped back from the corpse, still staring at his face. His eyes were open, staring blankly up into the night sky. All at once my stomach gave a flip.

"Your first battle, son?" he asked.

I nodded. "The Lieutenant, is he . . . is he . . . ?"

"He's fine. I think bullets bend around that man."

"But I saw somebody fall."

"Garrett caught one in the shoulder . . . not serious. Only two wounded, none killed."

"Where is the Lieutenant?" I asked.

"Inside the blockhouse," he answered, motioning to the front door of the building. "Go in and see for yourself."

As I walked I tried not to stare at the American prisoners, but the groaning of one of the men lying on the ground drew my gaze. Another soldier was binding his leg with a blood-stained cloth.

I opened the door and looked inside. It was brightly lit, with oil lamps positioned all around. Shelves crammed with provisions lined the walls from top to bottom and divided the large room. Barrels and sacks and wooden crates were piled in the aisles. It reminded me of Mr. McCann's store, before the war, except it was bigger, stocked with even more supplies.

"Hold the door!" a soldier called out.

I pulled it wide open and he exited the building carrying a half dozen muskets. No sooner had he passed than two more men came with similar loads. I found a broom and wedged it in against the door so it would remain open. Two more men came, carrying between them a wooden crate. Judging from the strained looks on their faces it must have been very heavy. Glancing around at the abundance I quickly realized there was no possible way that we could make off with all of these supplies.

In the corner, hovering over a desk, stood FitzGibbon and Merritt and another soldier. As I got closer I realized there was also a fourth man, dressed in a blue American uniform, who was sitting at the desk. Together the four of them were going through a large book. I moved closer— close enough to see and hear without being right there on top of them.

It quickly became apparent that the American was the supply officer for the blockhouse. He knew all of the contents of the building and where they were stored. FitzGibbon and Merritt were politely asking him questions and he was giving them answers. FitzGibbon would then have soldiers sent to those locations to remove the supplies. Mainly he was asking about weapons and ammunition and powder. When those had been found, FitzGibbon's inquiries turned to food items: flour, salt, whisky and tobacco. More soldiers were sent and more barrels and bags and crates were moved through the doors and outside.

"Thank you, sir, you have been both an officer and a gentleman," FitzGibbon said.

"And what will become of my men? Are you taking us back as prisoners?"

"That is not my intent. I am prepared to offer a proposal. We require assistance to transport these provisions back to our boats. Any man who carries his weight and acts with integrity will be released once we reach our vessels," FitzGibbon said. "You have my word."

The American rose to his feet. "And the wounded?"

"They will be allowed to remain. Do you have somebody who can tend to them?"

The American nodded. "I agree to your terms." He reached out his hand, FitzGibbon offered his, and they shook.

As they continued to stand there, making polite conversation, I was struck by the strangeness of the whole situation. This American officer was offering them assistance to take his supplies. Just a few minutes ago, they'd been trying to kill each other!

There was one other thing that struck me as odd. These two men, one dressed in a red uniform and the other in blue, could just as easily have been two old friends talking over the rail fence separating their properties— even two brothers, like my Pa and uncle. And yet the colour of their uniforms meant that in battle they were mortal enemies, each sworn to try to take the life of the other.

"May I be excused to tend to my men and inform them of your offer?" the American officer asked.

"Certainly."

They exchanged salutes and the officer was led away by two of our soldiers.

"It's a shame, isn't it, Tommy?" FitzGibbon said.

"What is?" I asked, surprised that he'd directed a question to me.

"All these supplies and we can't take all of them back across the river. There's much here that would help us and the families of the men along the Niagara."

"But we can take a lot."

"Quite a bit. Some provisions, weapons and ammunition. If we had more time, or more than one wagon—"

"There's a wagon?" I interrupted.

"Yes, and horses to pull it."

"But the wagon will never make it through that path," I said.

"You're right about that. We're going to travel along the main road back toward Lewiston as far as we can. If our advance guard meets no opposition we'll travel right to the sight of our first encounter with the militia. We'll pass the supplies from one man to the next along the trail down the cliff and to the boats. I just wish I had a second wagon so I could have taken away the two twelve-pound cannons and a six-pounder we found. I suppose it has to be enough to know that we've spiked them, ruined them so they'll never be capable of firing a shot."

"Ready to go, James," Merritt announced from the far end of the room. "The prisoners have been assembled, their wounded moved outside the walls, and the wagon is loaded with supplies and our wounded."

"Have you recalled the pickets from the road to Fort Niagara?" FitzGibbon asked.

"Being recalled now."

"Good. Would you please take the main party and

proceed down the road? Leave me three men and four horses and we'll set out once we've completed our work here. I have no doubt we'll overtake you long before you reach the boats."

"If you don't, I'll be back looking for you," Merritt said.

"Could I stay with you?" I asked FitzGibbon.

"It would be safer if you were with the main party."

"I'll stay out of the way," I pleaded.

FitzGibbon didn't answer immediately.

"Well, James?" Merritt asked. "Is he staying with you or coming with me?"

FitzGibbon smiled. "Leave a fifth horse behind."

"Thank you!" I cried. "Thank you!"

"Make good speed, William. I'll be done in thirty minutes and be by your side in less than forty."

Merritt left and we were alone again.

"Let's get started," FitzGibbon said. "Tommy, I want you to pick up an axe and smash open all those barrels in the back. Be careful, though, they're filled with whisky."

"But wouldn't it be better to destroy other things . . . food and clothing and blankets?" I suggested, gesturing to the still crammed shelves.

"That we are, Tommy," he answered. "The whisky is just the best available fuel for the fire."

"Fire?"

"Yes, we're burning this blockhouse to the ground."

*　　*　　*

FITZGIBBON, myself and two soldiers flew through the stores, smashing open the barrels of whisky. The air stank with the pungent smell of the alcohol. More than once one of the soldiers commented on the waste we were perpetrating. At first, I thought he meant setting fire to all the supplies, but really he meant the whisky spilling all over the floor.

At the edges of the spilled whisky we placed black gunpowder, the bags torn open to allow the powder to spill out. Next, scraps of paper and clothing, ripped into shreds, were thrown around the room.

"Well, here we go," FitzGibbon said.

He picked up one of the oil lamps and threw it toward a pile of alcohol-soaked cloth. The glass smashed noisily and the flames flashed free, catching the scraps instantly. A line of flames ran across the floor, seeking the spilled liquid. Although we were clear across the room, the resulting *whoosh* and rush of hot air shot back at us. I watched with fascination as the veins of fire raced around the room.

"It's caught. We'd better get outside before any of the powder ignites," FitzGibbon suggested.

I'd forgotten all about that. The four of us rushed out the door and to the soldier who was waiting, musket in hand, watching both the horses and the roadway in both directions. We all climbed on the mounts and moved to the gate. I couldn't help but think that this was the second time I'd stolen an American horse. I guess they couldn't hang me more than once anyway.

Looking back at the blockhouse there was nothing to see except a dim light shining through the one window facing our way.

"Are you sure it caught?" one of the men asked.

"Oh, it caught for sure," another answered. "It'll just take a few—"

His words were cut off by a massive explosion! My horse cried out and reared up on its hind legs. As I struggled to regain control there was a second explosion, louder than the first, followed almost immediately by what felt like a shower of hail. The force of the explosion had hurled debris into the air. My horse bucked again and rocketed forward through the gate, galloping wildly for a few seconds before I finally reined it in and it came to a halt.

I turned back toward the blockhouse. The entire roof was gone, blown up, and monstrous flames shot up into the sky. It was an amazing sight! The closest thing I could even imagine was the description of Hell's fires I'd heard from the minister's pulpit in church.

"What a glorious explosion!" FitzGibbon yelled from atop his horse. "That would have been heard from the Falls all the way to Fort George and beyond! Now we have to make haste. I'd prefer not to be here when they come to see what happened."

I brought my horse over to where he and the other men waited and together we charged down the road, to catch the rest of the men, find the boats and get back to Canada.

CHAPTER SEVEN

"SO HOW are you doing, Tommy?"

I recognized FitzGibbon's voice and quickly spun around. He was standing at the edge of the field—the field I'd spent the better part of three days harvesting.

"I'm doing fine," I answered. "Fine . . . and you?"

"I'm well. Mr. DeCew informs me that you've been working very hard."

I nodded my head slightly but didn't answer. I had been working hard. Almost as hard as Mr. DeCew, who was working well into the night to grind grain at the mill. I understood that the plan all along had been for me to stay at the DeCews' and work in the fields until it was safe for me to return home, but somehow, after the expedition across the river to the States, I thought that I'd proven something—that maybe I belonged with the Bully Boys. But the morning after we returned to Canadian soil, FitzGibbon had arranged to have me brought back to the DeCew farm. That was two weeks ago. Since then I'd worked hard, eaten well, slept solidly through the nights and spent a lot of time wondering about things. What was happening back at my farm? What was my Ma thinking? How was she managing? Where was Pa? And what adventure was FitzGibbon undertaking now—without me.

If being on the farm was hard before, it was doubly difficult now. Before, I could only imagine what it was like to be in the saddle or in the field fighting the Americans. Now I knew. I'd had a taste of honey and knew how sweet it was.

"Are you interested in a little ride?" FitzGibbon asked.

I had to fight the urge to shout out 'Yes!'

"Where?" I asked instead, as casually as I could.

"I'm leading a small party of men. We're heading south toward the Falls. I think our route might just pass to the west of Queenston."

"You're going by my home, by my farm?" I couldn't even pretend not to be excited.

"Do you think you can tear yourself away from the harvest long enough to come with me?"

I tossed the ear of corn I was holding into the basket. "Let me just go up to the house and tell Mrs. DeCew and—"

"All done. Your steed awaits," FitzGibbon said, bowing gracefully from the waist.

I looked past him, beyond the edge of the field. Two of his men—McAdams and Jamison—were standing there along with five horses. One of the horses was my grey, and I was happy to see her. They hadn't left her here when I was dropped off. I was told it was far too risky to have her in the barn on the off chance that an American patrol might come this far and find her and demand to know how she got there. I'd woken up in the middle of the night more than once thinking about being hanged as a horse thief—a double horse thief! Of course the second steed, the one I'd ridden away from the American blockhouse, had been left with the prisoners when we boarded the boats back for Canada. I can't say that I was sorry to see the end of that horse. He was bad-tempered and tried to throw me more than once as we'd thundered along the road to catch up with Merritt and the men. Maybe the horse had simply been shaken and spooked by the explosion, but I knew I preferred my grey.

Of course, the other image that kept me from going to sleep some nights was of that American soldier lying there on the ground, dead, his eyes open and staring. I wondered who he was, where he was from. Was he somebody's husband, or brother? Maybe he was even a father, although he was so young that if he'd had any children they would have just been babies. How awful to have your Pa die before you even really knew him . . . to not have any memories of him except for what people told you. At least I was old enough to remember my Pa if . . . I stopped myself. There was no point in going there again and again. Did that American's family even know yet what had happened to him? How long would it be before we knew if something had happened to Pa . . . I had to stop myself again.

We walked up and the two men offered a wave and greetings. We all climbed up onto our horses. I reached down and gave the grey a scratch behind the ears. I'd thought about naming her—I'd had a lot of time to think about such things as I was picking corn—but she really wasn't mine to name.

"Out in front about a hundred paces . . . no more than two turns in the road ahead," FitzGibbon ordered his men.

"Yes, sir," one of them replied and they started off ahead of us.

"I want you to lead the pack horse," the Lieutenant said to me.

I looked at the horse. It was heavily loaded down with sacks.

"How long are we going for?" I asked. It looked as though we had enough supplies to last a month.

"Not long. We're dropping these off along the way. That's why you're leading the pack animal. Most of what's strapped to the horse belongs to you."

"Me?" Now I was even more confused.

"Flour. Three bags. It's your payment for working in the fields for Mr. DeCew. We're going to be leaving the bags at your farm."

I smiled, then I knew how much it would mean to my Ma. I wondered if my family would be happier to see me or the supplies. I was pretty certain which they needed the most.

FitzGibbon gave his horse a gentle kick and started off. I leaned back and grabbed the reins of the second horse, urging both on to catch up to the Lieutenant. I slowed my horse as I reached his side.

We rode along, side by side in silence. Occasionally, when the trail reached a long straight stretch, I could see the other two men up ahead of us, but for the most part they were out of sight. I knew they were up front as scouts to warn us of any approaching danger.

"You must be missing your mother," FitzGibbon said.

"A lot. And my sisters. I've even been missing my brother . . . and I didn't think that would be possible."

"It's hard to be away from people you love." He paused. "I know about that." FitzGibbon reached a hand into an inside pocket and pulled something out. "Here," he said handing it to me.

It was a small portrait of a woman . . . a very pretty woman. The picture was behind a piece of glass and the backing was a thick strip of leather.

"Her name is Mary. Mary Haley."

"She's very . . ." I stopped. Maybe I shouldn't be saying anything.

"Yes, she is very beautiful. And she has agreed to become my wife."

"Congratulations."

Carefully I handed him back the portrait. He looked at it again before tucking it back into his jacket. I noticed this time that he had placed it in a pocket over his heart. I had to smile.

*　　*　　*

WE TRAVELLED through the better part of the morning before we stopped for lunch, a quick bite grabbed off to the side of the trail. We'd seen nothing all day except birds in the sky and the back end of two deer disappearing among the trees.

"This must be looking familiar to you," FitzGibbon said.

I nodded. "I know the area pretty well. I helped out with a barn raising at a farm not far from here."

"What was the name of the people?" FitzGibbon asked.

"Watson."

"Robert and Edna Watson?" FitzGibbon asked.

"Yes, that's them. Do you know them?"

"Not them, but I know the farm . . . or what's left of the farm."

"I don't understand."

"The house and the barn were burned down."

"Who would—"

"Dr. Cyrenius Chapin," he said, spitting the words as though they were poison. "He and his men. They're far worse than any American. In fact, even the Americans dislike him. I understand they call his men 'The Forty Thieves.'"

"But why would he do that to the Watsons?" I was remembering what nice people they were, and that day, almost two years ago, when my family and every family from all around had worked to raise that building.

"Chapin hardly needs a reason to plunder or take prisoners or burn homes. He would claim that the Watsons were providing aid, but that would be nothing more than an excuse to be a—"

He stopped talking as both of us noticed our scouts coming back toward us down the path. They were moving fast.

"Sir, American cavalry," one of them exclaimed excitedly as he brought his steed to a halt right in front of us.

"At least ten men," the other added.

"How far? How fast?" FitzGibbon asked.

"A few hundred paces . . . moving slowly."

"We have to get back to the path we just crossed,"

FitzGibbon ordered. "Tommy, take the lead. If we move quickly we can still avoid being detected. Now go!"

I spun my horse and dragged the second one behind me. I glanced nervously over my shoulder, relieved to see only the three familiar faces and nothing else behind them on the path. We rounded two quick corners and came to the path, and I brought my horse to a stop. Directly in front of us was the longest and most open stretch of the trail we'd travelled along. If we rode hard we could probably get to cover on the other side before the Americans got to this side of the clearing. Off to the right the path led to Queenston and Fort George beyond it. To the left were the cliffs of the escarpment. I knew this area well.

"Everybody to the left," FitzGibbon ordered.

"But that's a dead-end," I objected. "There's no way to get a horse down from there except by turning back down the path again. There's only one way in or out."

"If need be, could we get down the escarpment without the horses?" FitzGibbon asked.

"Sure, there are spots we could climb down," I assured him.

"Good. Let's proceed up the path then. I'm gambling that the Americans are going back to the town or to the

Fort, and the one way they won't go is farther up the escarpment."

"And if they do?" I asked.

"Then we make a stand. At least we'll have the high ground. And if we have to, we abandon the horses."

He made sense, I thought.

"Tommy, you know the way."

I turned my horse up the much narrower path, and the pack horse followed. I wanted to move quickly but the path was both rough and rutted in places where the fast run-off after countless storms had washed away parts of the trail, leaving behind a mixture of loose rocks and stones. I ducked down to get underneath some low-hanging branches. I didn't remember the path being so enclosed by trees, but then again I'd only ever travelled it on foot.

In fact, I'd only been up this path a half dozen times in my life—the last time three years before—but I remembered it well. It was fairly short, overgrown and then opened up to a wider spot at the top to offer a view for a long way in all directions. The last time I'd gone to the top was with my cousin, Susan. She'd practically leaned over the edge of the rocks while I hung back. I didn't like heights, but I didn't want my cousin—my younger, female cousin—to know I was afraid of something she wasn't.

Instead, I convinced her that I wanted to explore the caves that riddled the cliffs of the escarpment.

This time we would all have to make a point of staying away from the edge. No only could you *see* a long way from up there, you could *be seen* from a great distance as well.

"We can't go any farther," I said, bringing the two horses to a stop. "We'll run out of cover soon."

FitzGibbon reined in his horse as did Jamison, who was leading McAdam's mount. McAdams was nowhere to be seen. The two men dismounted and I did the same.

"Join McAdams," FitzGibbon ordered, and Jamison walked back down the trail.

"What do we do if they do come up this path?" I asked.

He shrugged. "What we have to do. You're sure there's no other way down from here for the horses?"

"None, it's pretty steep, even for a climber, and there are a couple of caves—"

"Caves?"

"Lots of them," I answered.

"Are any big enough to hide five horses?"

"Not even close. Some of them are so small that I'd have to hold my breath to get through the tight spots." I paused. "But there is an overhang."

"Where?"

"Right by the top."

"And could we get the horses down there?" FitzGibbon asked.

"I . . . I don't know . . . maybe . . . I think there's a side trail, but . . ."

I stopped as Jamison and McAdams came running back up the path. I swallowed hard and said a silent prayer that they were just rushing back with the good news that it was safe for us to return—but from their hurried pace I knew that wasn't likely.

"They've turned up the trail," Jamison said, panting for breath.

"You'd better show us that overhang, Tommy," FitzGibbon said.

I nodded my head in agreement and started to lead my horses away quickly. The men followed closely behind me. We broke through the last of the trees and the path opened up to brush and bare rock. If we couldn't get down to the overhang we'd at least have to get back down the path far enough to reach cover again—not with the hope of remaining unseen, but in order to take shelter when the shooting began.

I felt that same feeling in the pit of my stomach I'd felt the night we crossed the Niagara, standing in the dark, waiting. Part of me wanted desperately to be someplace else, and another part wouldn't have me anywhere else in the whole wide world.

I came close to the edge and couldn't help but look down the side of the cliff. I leaned away from the edge and then climbed down from my horse. I trusted my own feet more than I trusted the horses'. I led the horses over to the rough path leading down the side to the overhang. It was steeper and rougher than I recalled. I could get down, but could the horses?

I started down and a small shower of rocks skidded down before me. I slowed my pace. If I tripped it would be one thing, but if either of the horses slipped they would fall right on top of me. I heard rocks sliding behind me but didn't dare look back. The path flattened out. We were still well above the bottom of the cliff.

Right ahead, jutting out from the rock face, was the overhang. Covering it like a curtain were vines growing down from above, almost to the ground. This made for better cover but meant I couldn't see into it. Was it really big enough to hide four men and five horses? I remembered it as being large, but that was three years ago, and things I'd always thought were large had gotten smaller and smaller since I'd grown.

Holding the reins and the lead for the pack horse in one hand, I reached out with the other and swept the covering away. With a sense of relief I realized that the space was just large enough for us to fit into. I stepped forward, pushing aside the vines. My horse balked at the entrance and I had to coax her forward. Once she'd come completely through, I let go of her reins and went back, moving the vines aside once more to create an opening for the pack horse to follow in behind. Within less than a minute all the men and their horses had also taken refuge. When the last horse entered I felt a release, as though a weight that had been sitting on my chest had suddenly been lifted.

It was a lot cooler there than on the path, exposed to the sun. Above our heads was solid rock, close enough in places that I could reach up and touch it. The ground was mainly rock and mud, with a few small puddles in places. My horse lapped up a drink from one of the puddles. While the vines had looked like a solid curtain from the outside there were actually lots of gaps and spaces that I could look through.

"Here," Jamison said handing me a feedbag.

"We're going to feed the horses now?" I asked in amazement. If we were discovered, we wouldn't want to waste time taking off the feedbags before we made a run for it.

"Best time in the world. A horse wearing a feedbag around its muzzle isn't about to snort or make noises that might give us away," he explained.

I put the bag on my grey while he did the same with the pack horse. I'd just finished when FitzGibbon motioned for me to come over.

"I'm sure you've fired a gun many a time, Tommy."

"Sure, I used to go hunting all the time."

"Good. Here you go," he said as he pulled a rifle from a holster on the side of his horse. "You might need this." FitzGibbon shook his head ruefully. "I was just telling you how I wanted to keep you safe and now I'm handing you a weapon. I'd better be careful what I say to you in the future."

I took the rifle from him. I was a good shot, and I liked having a gun in my hands.

"What sort of things have you shot before?" he asked.

"Rabbits. I've been shooting rabbits since I was seven years old. And I've bagged a few deer, I once got a ten-pointer buck, and raccoons, and—"

"You've never shot at a man before, have you?" FitzGibbon asked, cutting me off.

"Of course not!"

"It's no different than shooting at any other animal, at least until you hit it. You shoot an animal and you change the animal's life. You shoot a man and you change the lives of two men—the man you shot, and you." He paused. "Don't shoot unless I do. I hope we won't have to, but if we do, you take aim straight at the chest, hold her steady so she doesn't jump up on you, and then you fire. Can you do that, Tommy?"

I nodded my head. Despite the coolness of our surroundings I felt a sudden rush of sweat. My hands, holding onto the rifle, were wet. I wiped first one, and then the other, on my pants.

Suddenly, we heard the sound of hoofbeats above our heads.

"Tommy," FitzGibbon whispered, "you said there are caves as well?"

"Lots of them," I whispered back.

"And you said they weren't big enough for the horses, but some are big enough for a man or two, aren't they?"

"Some aren't that wide but they go on for a long way. We could all fit in one of the big ones. There's one that goes all the way from the top down to the side of the cliff," I answered.

"So you're saying it has two openings," FitzGibbon whispered.

There was a slight echo to his whisper. I knew that his voice wouldn't travel far—not to the Americans at the top of the cliff—but still it made me nervous.

Silently I nodded my head in response.

A smile crossed his face. "I have an idea," FitzGibbon said. "Tie up the horses."

The five steeds were secured to the exposed tree roots that poked through the back of the overhang. I wondered what he had in mind. FitzGibbon put a finger to his lips to show he wanted silence. He then motioned for us to follow as he first poked his head out and then exited through the vine curtain. Jamison followed right behind, then me, and then McAdam.

I looked up. The overhang still masked us sufficiently that we weren't visible to anybody at the top. FitzGibbon moved slowly, his back to the rock face, glancing forward and then overhead to make sure he still had cover. He was moving toward the very top of the cliff, to where the American soldiers were waiting.

I could picture them up there, either still atop their horses or standing beside them. They would be looking down on the surrounding countryside, searching for

British soldiers. It was a good view from the top and they'd be able to see a long way. I could understand why they went up there. What I couldn't understand was why we were going there now. Wasn't the whole idea to hide from them?

I stumbled and a couple of small rocks rolled noisily down the slope. FitzGibbon and Jamison turned around abruptly. Jamison shot me a dirty look and FitzGibbon put a finger to his lips again to signal silence. I shrugged my shoulders by way of apology. I had to keep my mind on my feet instead of trying to figure out what we were going to do. Actually there was no point in even wasting any more thought on that. It was obvious what we were going to do. We were going to attack the Americans.

CHAPTER EIGHT

I FROZE IN my steps as I heard the whinnying of a horse. If I could hear it, maybe the Americans could hear it too and they'd discover us, and—and then I realized it wasn't one of *our* horses I was hearing. It had to be one of *their* animals. The sound was coming from the top of the cliff. That removed the small doubt I had that they were still up there. In my heart I'd hoped they had simply ridden up, looked out, turned around and were now gone.

McAdams came up from behind and tapped me on the shoulder, indicating that I should move on. I started climbing again and soon was right behind Jamison. There were plenty of handholds and the rocks were solid—no loose stones to trip on or kick noisily down the slope. It was awkward to climb with the rifle on my back, and the barrel grazed against the rock as I lifted myself over the lip of a small overhang.

FitzGibbon and Jamison were sheltered inside the mouth of a cave. Looking higher, beyond them, I saw the very peak of the cliff. If one of the Americans had looked down just then I'd have been seen. I quickly moved to the shelter of the cave alongside the others. Within seconds McAdams was with us as well.

A horse cried out again, and then I heard voices. Laughter. We were that close.

"Do you know this cave?" FitzGibbon asked me in a whisper.

I shrugged. It had been years since I'd been there.

"There's fresh air blowing out of the entrance," he said. "It must lead somewhere."

Then I remembered. "I've been in this cave before. This is the one that twists around until it comes out just below the top."

"Show me," FitzGibbon said.

I started to climb out of the cave but he grabbed me by the arm. "No, show me this way," he said pointing toward the darkness.

I didn't want to get any closer to the Americans than I already was. "It's very tight. I don't know if we can get through with our guns."

"We'll leave the weapons here."

"But . . ." If getting closer to them was something I didn't want to do, getting closer and leaving our weapons behind seemed like an even worse idea.

FitzGibbon handed Jamison his rifle and reluctantly I passed mine to McAdams.

I ventured farther into the cave. Almost instantly I had to duck down to get beneath a rock jutting down from the roof. The cave took a sharp twist to the right and then started to climb. As soon as I made the turn, the light coming in from the entrance was blocked and it became dim, almost dark.

As I started to climb the steep incline I remembered how black it had got the time I'd been through the cave before; how the walls had closed in around me in the growing darkness and how much I'd wished I'd had a candle with me. I sure wanted one now.

As I continued the slow climb, the cave grew steadily darker, but my eyes seemed to grow accustomed to the change. In truth, there wasn't much to look at but the walls, and they were only inches away in all directions. At least this time I didn't have to worry about getting stuck. I'd made it through before so I knew I could get through again . . . so long as I hadn't grown so much over the past years that I was now too big to fit . . . A cold sweat started trickling down my sides and I stopped. But as hard as it had been to climb up, I knew it would be almost impossible to back down.

"Keep moving," FitzGibbon said softly, reaching up and tapping me on the bottom of my left shoe.

I pressed forward. My fear of getting trapped was growing, but it was still less than my fear of disappointing FitzGibbon. Another twist . . . I didn't want to go up or around any farther . . . but wait, there was more light now. I could see things more clearly. We were nearing the opening at the top. I climbed up and crawled around the bend. It was suddenly much brighter. Looking up, I saw the end of the cave and the blue sky beyond it. With renewed energy I scrambled the rest of the way. The space became much wider and it was easier to move. I stopped a dozen feet short of the opening. FitzGibbon came up beside me and then moved past me. He, too, stopped just short of the entrance.

Carefully I moved up beside him. I opened my mouth to say something but stopped; I could clearly hear voices and laughter flowing into the mouth of the cave. FitzGibbon poked his head out. He grabbed onto a jagged piece of rock and leaned forward, twisting his head so he could see up. If anybody at the top, just a couple of feet away, had looked down they couldn't have helped but see him. How fast could we get back down to the other end? I was sure I could move a whole lot faster knowing there were men with guns after me, but maybe not fast enough. And even if I could get to the other end, they'd still be up top, looking down, ready to fire as I tried to run to the overhang.

FitzGibbon swung back into the cave—thank God.

"No good," he whispered. "I could hear them but they weren't saying anything worth listening to."

"Maybe we should get back down before they hear us," I whispered back.

He nodded. "Yes we should—" Then he stopped abruptly in mid-sentence. Had he heard something that I hadn't?

"Or maybe they *should* hear us," FitzGibbon said. "How loud can you yell?"

"What?"

"Come," he whispered as he grabbed me by the arm and led me to the very edge of the cave.

I leaned slightly back and away from the drop, the long drop, from the cave down to the bottom of the cliff.

"When I start yelling, you yell too," FitzGibbon said.

"But—"

"Just do what I say," he interrupted.

I started to nod my head in agreement when FitzGibbon suddenly shrieked and whooped at the top of his lungs. I jumped as the sound echoed through and out of the cave. It was an incredible noise. It didn't sound like one man, or two, or even ten—it sounded like an entire tribe of Indians right there surrounding me! I added my voice and suddenly two entire tribes of natives were yelling and screaming and shrieking.

FitzGibbon abruptly stopped yelling and put a hand over my mouth to silence me. There was no sound. No voices. Not the neighing of horses or laughter or even the sound of birds singing. Silence.

Slowly FitzGibbon inched to the mouth of the cave. He leaned out and looked up. Then he started to climb out and up. I rushed forward to the entrance just in time to see him above me, first peeking over the top and then climbing right up and out of sight. His head soon reappeared over the edge.

"It's all right, Tommy," he said, laughing. "Come on up."

Carefully, making sure I had secure foot- and hand-holds, I climbed up the few feet separating me from the top. FitzGibbon stood alone. In his hand was a canteen.

"This is all that's left of those Americans. Probably dropped it as they bumped into each other trying to get away."

He opened the lid, turned the canteen upside down and poured out the contents. It was obvious from the strong smell that it had held whisky and not water. The pungent smell of the alcohol took me back to the block-house across the Niagara.

"That was quite amusing," FitzGibbon said. "You have a pretty good Indian war cry."

"I do?"

"You have to remember that the Americans are terri-fied of the natives, just terrified. Are you afraid of Indians?" he asked.

"I don't know . . . maybe a little, I guess," I admitted reluctantly. I really hadn't had much to do with the Indians. I knew there was a group who camped each summer on the stream not far from our house, but I'd never even seen them, let alone talked to any of them.

"Most of the Americans are more than just a little scared. They're downright terrified. They think they're going to be scalped or tortured. They tell stories, but most of that is just make-believe. So, can you get us back down to the others without going back through the cave? I really don't fancy tight little spaces like that."

"Sure, we can go this way," I said.

"Lead away."

We started down from the top. I was looking for the place where we'd originally gone down with the horses.

"Do you know who started the practice of scalping the dead?" FitzGibbon asked.

"Not really."

"White settlers."

"You mean Indians don't scalp people?" I asked.

"I didn't say that. Some tribes do it, but it wasn't a practice that was invented by the natives. I think the real reason the Americans fear the natives so much is because of all the terrible things they've done to them. One of the greatest men I ever met was Tecumseh. He's a man of integrity, honesty and intelligence. In fact, most of the ignorant savages I've met speak the King's English, are as white as cream and were born in the Old World. When we get back to camp I'll arrange to take you one night to the camp of one of our allies. Maybe the Caughnawagas."

"Will we have to travel far to get there?"

He chuckled. "No more than a few miles. They usually camp close by our site."

"I didn't know that."

"Always. We work together. Captain Dominique Ducharme has one hundred and eighty Caughnawagas under his command, while Captain William Kerr has some two hundred tribesmen from the Six Nations. Without them this war would have been settled long ago, and not in our favour."

"I didn't even know there were that many Indians around here," I said.

"There are many, but our ranks have been swelled by our native brothers from throughout Upper Canada as well as the northern States."

"Even Indians from the United States are on our side?" I questioned.

"That's where Tecumseh and his people are from. You have to understand, Tommy, that the British have perpetrated their share of injustices against the Indians, but prior to this war the American army launched countless attacks that slaughtered thousands upon thousands of

Indians, burned villages, forced them to leave their lands. Things the natives will never forget. And that is why they are on our side. We are the enemy of their enemy, and thus we are allies. I just pray that the King will recognize and reward their deeds when we finally drive the Americans back across the river."

The rocks under my feet slipped and I scrambled to regain my balance. Hitting the flat I saw Jamison and McAdams ahead. They were standing outside the vine-covered overhang and waved to us.

"I wish you'd have let us know what you were up to before you did it, Lieutenant," Jamison said.

"When you started screaming you nearly scared the daylights out of me!" McAdams added. "You haven't any idea how loud that echoes on down through the cave!"

FitzGibbon just smiled.

"And then when the screaming stopped we heard those Americans charging down the hill like they were being chased by the Devil himself. You should have heard them! Screaming, yelling, cursing, their horses snorting and hooves pounding against the rock! I don't know how they managed to get down without half of them going over the edge!"

FitzGibbon started to laugh again, that loud, explosive laughter that made everybody within earshot start to smile and then laugh along with him. It dissolved the tension that had been gripping my stomach like a fist and I broke into laughter as well.

"I suppose we'd better get going before they get down to the fort and report the hundreds of Indians up here. You never know, they might actually find the nerve to round up a few hundred soldiers and come back!"

*　　*　　*

I DIDN'T know what I was most pleased about: seeing the last of those Americans or starting to see the familiar sights that marked the approach to our land. We passed between two large piles of stones that my Pa and uncle and I had taken out of one of our fields last year. My Pa always joked that with all the rocks we pulled out each spring you would have thought we were planting stone seeds. If the war hadn't come I would have spent a good part of that summer making those piles into fences. That and felling trees and pulling the stumps to make our fields bigger.

Up ahead, grazing peacefully, were a dozen of our sheep . . . and our plough horse . . . and in the distance I could see the tip of our barn. After hearing about the Watsons' barn, I was more than a little relieved to see it. Off to the side was the little plot of land where my grandparents were buried, and then I saw my favourite climbing tree, and . . . my Ma was standing beside it.

CHAPTER NINE

"MA!" I screamed at the top of my lungs as I spurred my horse to race toward her.

She dropped the basket she was holding and ran to me. I brought the horse to a stop, its hooves throwing up clumps of dirt, leaped down to the ground and threw my arms around her.

"Tommy, Tommy," she whispered as she wrapped me tightly in a hug.

She started to cry and I could feel her entire body shaking. I released my grip on her but her arms remained tightly around me.

"It's okay, Ma . . . I'm okay."

She sobbed even louder. "I know . . . I know," she managed to choke out.

I heard the footfalls of FitzGibbon's horse right behind me and I felt almost embarrassed as my mother continued to cling to me. I tried to console her, to make her see it was all right. Why was she crying so much? I was right here and everything was all right. I patted her on the back . . . when had she become so small? It had been almost two years since the first time we'd stood back to back and I was just a hair taller. Of course I'd kept growing since then— but she seemed so much smaller now, so thin. I couldn't have grown that much in just a few weeks.

"Good morning, ma'am," the Lieutenant announced.

She released her hold, slightly, and looked up at him, still atop his horse.

"My name is James Fitz—"

"I know who you are, Lieutenant FitzGibbon," my mother interrupted. "And for the first few days after my son was gone I wasn't too happy at the mention of your name."

I had to smile. There was a little taste of that fire that I knew was inside of her.

"I can understand your distress," he said. "It was with a

heavy heart that I had to ask your son to accompany me."

"Your heart was light compared to mine. You have no idea what it is like for a mother to be separated from her son."

"Indeed not, ma'am . . . although I know the pain I felt as a son separated from his mother." FitzGibbon dismounted.

"And I was angry," my mother continued. "Angry at your reasons for taking my son. Surely, I thought, the Americans would not be so mean-spirited or petty as to hunt down a mere boy." She paused. "But I was wrong on that count."

"They were here looking for me?" I asked.

She nodded her head. "A party of ten soldiers, one with his head bandaged and bloodied, came snooping around the farm. Apparently somebody in town is a traitor and told the Americans it was you who attacked their man."

"What happened when the soldiers came?" FitzGibbon asked.

"I told them it couldn't be my son Tommy because he hadn't left the farm for more than a week."

"And they believed you?" FitzGibbon asked.

"No, but they did believe their own man and his eyes."

"I don't understand," I said.

"I let them see my son."

"But how could you—" I started to say.

"My son, John . . . your brother . . . who told them he was Tommy. The two soldiers, the one with the bandaged head and one other, looked at him and said that he wasn't the one."

"Well done, ma'am, very well done indeed!" FitzGibbon exclaimed.

"And of course Mr. McCann swore up and down that he'd known my son since he was born, and that he was old but not senile and knew it wasn't Thomas." She paused. "What would they have done to my Tommy if they had found him?"

FitzGibbon did not answer immediately. "Perhaps they would have beaten him, or taken him prisoner and brought him back to the States."

My Ma reached out and took my hand in hers. "And we've seen what they've done to the farms of people they suspect of doing them harm." She shook her head. "I would never have believed that there were men capable of burning people out, stealing their possessions . . . if I hadn't seen it with my own eyes, or heard it from people who had seen it all happen."

"It has happened, although thank goodness not that often. Most of the soldiers, American and British and Canadian, are honourable people. There are always a few bad apples in every barrel, though, aren't there?" the Lieutenant said.

"Surely you can't mean to say that some of His Majesty's men have acted similarly?" my Ma questioned.

"I can only speak directly for my men. But I know of similar acts, the burning of homes on the American side. While they were done as acts of retribution for American atrocities on this side of the river, they still left innocents without shelter."

I couldn't imagine that FitzGibbon would ever order or allow such behaviour. He was a gentleman. Then I thought about our burning of the blockhouse. That was different, though . . . that was a military building, and not the house or barn of some poor homesteader.

"It will be so good to have Tommy back under our roof . . ." She paused, and the smile on her face faded as she looked up at FitzGibbon. "It is safe now . . . you are leaving him . . . aren't you?"

"I'm sorry, ma'am. He is here for the day, but I do not believe it would be safe to leave him here for—"

"I understand," she interrupted. "And I trust your judgment in these matters, Lieutenant."

"I think it would be best if he remained at a safe distance for the next month or so."

"But he is with us for the day?"

"The day and possibly the night. My men and I must go farther and there is no guarantee that we'll be back before nightfall."

"I wish you to encounter no problems, Lieutenant, but I hope you are delayed enough to allow him to spend one night in his own bed!"

"I'm afraid that wouldn't be advisable," FitzGibbon said.

"But I don't understand." I turned to FitzGibbon. "You said you might be gone until tomorrow."

"Regardless, your bed needs to stay unoccupied. You should sleep in the hayloft. You need to stay away from the house in case an American patrol returns this evening. I know it is a long shot, but—"

"We can't take that chance," my Ma said. "Not for Tommy and not for the rest of the family. He'll sleep in the hay tonight. Let's get up to the house . . . your brother and sisters will be so happy to see you! Lieutenant, can you join us for a cup of tea before you leave?"

"I'm afraid I have to decline your invitation. Perhaps another time. Tommy, I'm leaving you the supplies, but I have to take your grey with me."

"I thought you might." I knew that if soldiers came then I could easily hide in the hay or scoot out the back door and into the woods without being seen. But the horse would still be there in the barn where anybody could see it and maybe remember that it belonged to an American soldier.

"Where do you want these supplies, ma'am?" FitzGibbon asked.

"Supplies?"

"Everything on the horse is meant for your family. They're the wages your son has earned working on the DeCews' farm."

My Ma was more than just a little pleasantly surprised.

"Well, I'm glad to hear he's been working all this time and not trying to run off and be a soldier," she told the Lieutenant. "I know the young men are needed to fight, but they're needed on the farm, too."

I looked at FitzGibbon, who was looking down at the ground. I didn't want to lie to my Ma, but there was no way I wanted her to know anything about what else had transpired.

"But surely all these supplies can't be for us!" she exclaimed, once she'd had a look at the provisions.

"You can use what your family requires and offer some to others you know who might be in need," the Lieutenant said.

"Thank you," she said, taking his hands in hers.

"No need. Thanks goes to your son and to Mr. DeCew."

"And is that where my son will be going back to after he leaves?"

"Yes. That's where he'll spend his time until he returns home."

"That's so good . . . so good to know he's safe . . . especially after what's happened to his Pa."

CHAPTER TEN

MY HEART ROSE up into my throat. My Pa?

"He was wounded in battle," she said.

"Is he badly hurt?" I demanded.

"I was told he's going to be all right. I'm sorry . . . I didn't know how to tell you."

"Where is he?"

"In a field hospital near Burlington. At least that was where he was . . . but I was told almost a week ago, and he was wounded ten days before that, so I don't really know." Ma shook her head slowly. "I was told by Mr. McGregor and he was told by somebody else. That was all the information he had."

"But there must be some way to find out how he's doing and where he is," I said.

"Lieutenant?" my Ma asked FitzGibbon.

"I can make some inquiries, but it's very difficult . . . I'll try, when we get back to our camp tomorrow."

"Thank you, Lieutenant. I'd be most grateful and in your debt," she said.

"No ma'am, if I do a dozen favours for your family I will still remain in your debt. If it hadn't been for your son, I would have been killed or captured. You should be very proud of Tommy."

"I am . . . I always have been. He's a good boy . . . but he really isn't a boy any more, is he?"

I wasn't? It was only a few short weeks ago that she had told me that I was too young, just a boy, and there was no way I was going off to fight in any war.

"TOMMY!"

I recognized my sister Sarah's shrill call and turned around in time to see her and my brother John racing toward me. Behind them came the twins, moving as fast as their little legs would carry them. Sarah got close and then leaped the last three feet into my arms, nearly knocking me backwards as she wrapped her arms around me tightly.

"Lieutenant FitzGibbon, this is my sister Sarah, my brother John, and these two are nothing but trouble," I said, as the twins wrapped their arms around my legs.

My brother reached up to take off his hat and extended his free hand to shake FitzGibbon's.

"Honoured to meet you, sir," he mumbled, his eyes cast down to the ground.

"Pleased to meet you as well, John. I think I must owe you an apology, too. With me taking away Tommy it must have left you with a lot more work to do."

"Some," he answered, shuffling his feet. He looked uneasy.

"Some?" Ma said. "With both their Pa and Tommy gone he's been the man of the house, and he's been doing a wonderful job!"

John blushed slightly, but I also noticed him puff out his chest and he brought his eyes up off the ground.

"It was my pleasure to meet you all, but I'd better be off if I'm to have any chance of getting back by nightfall," FitzGibbon said. "If I'm not back by then you should just settle in for the night and not expect me until midday tomorrow. Do you think you can stand to have your brother around for a while?"

John smiled, and Sarah, who had just released her grip on me, grabbed one of my hands tightly. The twins, who I didn't think really understood what he meant, still caught the spirit of the moment and started laughing.

"Before I go, I was wondering if you had some butter I could buy from you," FitzGibbon asked.

"We have a lot of butter," my Ma answered. "We just made it this morning—but none that you can buy, only what one neighbour can give to another."

"That's a very generous offer, ma'am, but I'll be needing a fairly large amount."

"You will? How much?"

"I believe somewhere between twenty and forty pounds."

"Twenty to forty pounds!" she exclaimed. "That's far more than I can provide. Why in the name of goodness would you be needing twenty pounds of butter?"

"You might say I need it to get me into, and then back out of, a very slippery situation," FitzGibbon answered with a laugh.

"I don't have nearly that much . . . maybe five, or even

seven pounds. But whatever we have you may take, so long as you take it for free."

"Ma'am, I insist that I pay you for—"

"And I will not hear another word about payment," my Ma interrupted. "Do I make myself clear?" she said, and that determined look was in her eyes again.

FitzGibbon opened his mouth to argue, but he must have known by her expression that it would be pointless. "Thank you," he said, bowing gracefully from the waist. "Thank you very much."

*　　*　　*

I PULLED the covers up tightly against my face. It wasn't that I was cold—it was a warm evening—I just liked the smell. It was the blanket off my bed. Ma had found another one for John to use in bed tonight and given me this to take into the hayloft. I'd managed to hollow out a comfortable depression in the hay. An occasional piece of straw still poked through my clothes and into my skin, but it really wasn't that troubling. After all, I was far from drifting off to sleep anytime soon.

My mind was filled with the sights of the farm, talking to my sisters, my brothers, Ma . . . how could everything that I'd known my whole life seem so different after only a few short weeks?

I couldn't get either Sarah or the twins to go any more than a dozen feet away from me throughout the day or evening. And when I mentioned wanting something more to eat, or a drink, they all jumped up and ran to get it. Usually none of them would get me a glass of water if my hair was on fire.

And Ma. Her shoulders were all stooped over now. She looked older and tuckered out. I guess part of it was worry, both about Pa and me. And part of it was probably all the extra work she'd been doing. John had been working hard and doing lots of things, but I knew she'd taken more than her share of turns behind the plough and harvesting in the fields, as well as doing all the house-work.

There was also a difference in her voice, or maybe in the tone of her voice. She asked me for my opinion about things—which crops we should put in next year, where I thought we should try to sink a new well, and about the war. And when I spoke she listened to what I had to say, like I was . . . a grown-up! I couldn't help but smile . . . a smile that was quickly erased as my thoughts turned back to my Pa.

It was strange how nobody had talked much about him today. I wanted to talk more than a few times, but I didn't want to get anybody upset . . . especially when there really wasn't anything we could do anyway. Once the Lieutenant got me back to camp, then I was sure he could get some information about Pa and I'd get that information back to my family and . . . What was that? I heard something moving outside the barn.

I sat up and perked my ears to try and make out the sounds. Maybe it was American soldiers . . . no, that made no sense. They wouldn't be sneaking around on foot; I would have heard horses. It was probably just some animal skulking around the barn—a raccoon or skunk or even a fox. I was sure the chickens were all locked safely away in the barn here with me so there was nothing to be worried about. Then I heard the big barn door open.

"Tommy!" hissed out a voice, my brother's.

"I'm over here!" I called out.

"Where?"

I stood up. A greyish form moved through the darkness. "I'm here, Johnny."

He came toward me. I slumped back into my hollow in the hay, and he sat down beside me.

"You okay out here?" John asked.

"I've slept in worse places than this over the past few weeks." I didn't want to mention I'd also slept in far better . . . that fine room at the DeCew house, for one.

"I bet you have."

"But you didn't come out to ask me if the barn was okay," I said.

He didn't answer.

"I'm not letting you have the blanket. You should be grateful you're sleeping in the bed while I'm out here with the chickens and cows."

"I don't want the blanket . . . I want Pa to be home."

"Everybody wants him to come home, but—"

"I want to go and bring him home," John interrupted.

"Go where and bring him home?"

"To Burlington Bay. I'll take our wagon and bring him back."

"That's a long way off."

"I've been farther than that."

"When?"

"To York, by boat. Remember?"

"Of course I remember. You were only five years old and you were just luggage. Pa did everything. This is different. The farthest you've ever been by yourself is a dozen or so miles."

"I can still do it."

"It's not that easy. Even Pa couldn't get you to York now, what with the war and all. I doubt the Americans will even let you through their lines."

"I could sneak around them, or maybe just tell them I'm delivering some hay close by."

"It isn't that simple," I said. "Besides, he might not even be there any more."

"If he's not there then I'll just ask them where he's been moved to."

"They might not even know. It's all pretty confusing."

"Then I'd just keep looking until I found him," my brother argued.

"And then what? Do you think the Americans would just let you take him back through their lines?"

"Why wouldn't they?"

"Because he's the enemy," I explained.

"But he's wounded."

"But he still might have some information they want, or maybe he was involved in a battle that they fought and they want vengeance, or maybe they would take him prisoner because they're afraid his wounds will heal and he'll be able to fight them again. Maybe he's even getting better and is ready to go back into battle again. Had you thought of any of that?" I knew that I hadn't until I'd started arguing with him.

There was no answer, which of course meant he hadn't thought of it either.

"You can't go. Ma needs you here with her. It's bad enough with the two of us gone," I said.

"But we have to know how he is and to help him if he needs us. We have to!"

"You're right . . . but I'll take care of it."

"You?"

"That's right. Me."

There was a pause. He was thinking, and in the darkness I couldn't even try to read his face.

"Promise?" John asked.

"I give you my word," I said.

Now I had to figure out just how I could keep that promise.

CHAPTER ELEVEN

"SO, HOW was your visit with your family?" Lieutenant FitzGibbon asked as we rode along, side by side.

"It was nice . . . longer than I thought it was going to be, though."

FitzGibbon hadn't come back that first day, or even the next, as he'd said. Instead he'd arrived after dinner the day after that. On the one hand I was grateful for the extra time, but I'd been worried too—about what might have happened to him, and about what I'd do if the American soldiers did come back looking for me.

That first day home I pretty well stayed out of sight,

for that reason. But the second day I got up early and just started in with the chores, as usual. I worked hard—John was in charge and told me what work had to be done—until the Lieutenant just popped out of the forest and told me we had to get going. That didn't leave much time for goodbyes, but that was fine with me. I didn't much like that sort of thing anyway.

Ma hugged me just a bit tighter than she used to, and when I saw the tears in her eyes—and the weary, worried look on her face and John's—I almost wanted to stay. But I knew that would be dangerous, for all of us. The last thing my brother said to me, whispered softly so no one else could hear, was "Remember your promise."

Of course I remembered. That promise had kept me awake for hours the last two nights. Unfortunately my thinking hadn't brought me any closer to an answer. All the same obstacles that stood in the way of my brother also blocked me.

"Were you delayed because you ran into trouble?" I asked.

"More like an opportunity."

"And it involved butter?" The only thing that had occupied my thoughts more than worrying about Pa was wondering why FitzGibbon had wanted all that butter.

"Why yes, it did involve butter." He smiled. "A most delicious and useful thing it is. Useful to get into and out of tight places."

"What sort of places?"

"Places like Fort George," he said softly.

"Fort George!"

"Yes, lad. I spent a good part of yesterday at the fort among all those American soldiers. There are nearly three thousand of them stationed there."

"But how . . . why? Were you captured?"

"If I had been, I would not be here with you today."

"But . . . how did you get away?"

FitzGibbon let out a loud laugh. "Why I just strolled right out through the front gate. The same way I walked in." He laughed again. "And when I left I had a tidy sum of their coin jingling in my pocket. After all, I gave them a very good price on the butter I was selling."

"You went into the fort to sell them butter?"

"I had to. It was the best way I could figure to get into the fort and do a little bit of spying."

"What if they had discovered it was you? They would have taken you prisoner."

"I would not have been a prisoner for long, Tommy."

"You mean you had a plan to escape . . . like a secret passage or something?"

He shook his head. "I would not have been a prisoner for long because they would have hanged me."

I gasped.

"They take soldiers prisoners. Spies they hang, and as soon as I'd exchanged my uniform for the disguise, I was a spy."

"Then you shouldn't have gone. You shouldn't have risked it."

"I had no choice. It was far too dangerous to send anybody else, and we needed to gather information." He smiled. "Besides, it was a jolly good laugh . . . and I knew it would make for a fine story. Do you want to hear it?"

"Of course!" I exclaimed.

"I got the idea a few days ago. If somebody had the freedom to wander among the Americans, right in the fort, maybe they could find out all sorts of interesting information. I hoped the Americans would feel safe and free to talk."

"And did they?"

"They chattered away like magpies!" he exclaimed. "But let's not put the cart before the horse. Let me start this story from the beginning."

I'd heard FitzGibbon tell enough stories to know that not only was it going to be a wonderful tale, but it would probably fill all the time between here and the camp.

"I bought butter from loyal farmers along the route. I had close to forty pounds in my cart," he began. "Then, dressed in my disguise, I approached the main gate of the fort."

"I would have been terrified," I said. Even thinking about it gave me that same weak feeling in the knees I always got when I looked down from a high place.

"I should hope so! I was so scared that I could almost feel my knees knocking together," FitzGibbon said.

"You were scared?" I'd imagined there was nothing he was afraid of.

"Of course. Only a fool does not get scared, and only a liar claims not to."

"I just thought . . . the way you act . . . the things you do . . ."

"That I don't feel afraid?" he asked.

I nodded my head.

"I was once told that the difference between a brave man and a coward is not how he feels, but what he does despite those feelings. I believe that to be true." He paused. "I don't think I have ever entered a battle without my stomach being gripped with fear. In fact, I don't believe I would trust a man who did *not* feel afraid."

Well, FitzGibbon could certainly trust *me*. I felt nervous just *hearing* about him walking into the fort.

"So, picture me as a farmer, pushing my cart, dressed in old clothes, entering through the front gate of the fort."

"Weren't you concerned that the Americans would just take all your butter without paying?"

"That wasn't a big worry . . . not compared to hanging! I trusted that they would act honourably."

"Huh! I was there at the general store when they just barged in and were going to take what they wanted without paying. And I've heard about soldiers going to farms and robbing the homesteaders."

"That's all true, Tommy. All armies, including the British, have their share of liars, thieves and robbers. But most of the Americans aren't any different from our men, and they act honourably. I was counting on that."

"So they let you just walk into the fort?"

"Actually, it was more like I limped in. I pretended to have a lame leg to explain why I was not in the service of one of the armies. As I pushed my cart I leaned against it to take the weight off my bad leg. And they didn't just let me stroll in. The sentries stopped me and asked all sorts of questions. But once they found out I had butter for sale, and at a good price, they opened the gate."

I shook my head.

"So I made my way across the parade grounds, looking for the supply officer for the fort. And as I walked I talked to different men. Just being friendly like, striking up a conversation, asking them questions and such."

"What sort of questions?"

"Things like where they were from and how long they had been away from home," he answered. "Important things like that."

"But why are those things important?"

"A man who has come farther and been away longer is most likely to be most unhappy. And an unhappy soldier is not a good soldier. He is more likely to not want to fight when a battle is going against him, more likely to turn and run, maybe even desert."

"And?"

"And many of these Americans have come from far away. Some from way down south . . . which is good news for us. Once the weather changes, many of these men, unused to and unprepared for a good, hard Niagara winter, will find their minds drifting back to the warmth of the south. Where the mind goes, the body is most likely to follow."

"Did you learn anything else?" I asked.

"I learned that there are fewer men at the fort than we thought. There are only twenty-eight hundred men stationed there."

"How did you learn that?" I couldn't imagine him counting them.

"I asked. Their supply officer provided me with the numbers so I could figure out how much butter and milk and meat they would need. I told him I could get everything he required at a cheaper price than he was paying . . . and hinted that we could split the profit without anybody being the wiser."

I just shook my head again.

"I had no more than met the man when I realized he was a chap of very little brain, and even less integrity. As soon as I told him I could supply more than just butter, and at a good price, I knew he would let me in on more than he should . . . and he did. What really baited the hook for him was my promise to bring all the supplies right to the fort so he wouldn't have to go outside and try to locate them himself." He paused. "You see, this supply officer lives in deadly fear of going beyond the walls of the fort. It seems that he has heard rumours about a British officer ... a man who is reputed to be pure evil ... a fellow by the name of FitzGibbon. He told me a few tales, and I have to admit that I began to be afraid of this FitzGibbon fellow myself." The Lieutenant burst out into a loud and boisterous laugh.

"But how could you just sit there with a straight face and listen to stories like that?" I asked.

"Oh, I didn't just listen. I made up a few of my own," he said softly. "By the time I was through describing some of the things I'd heard about this devil FitzGibbon, I think that poor supply officer wanted to hide under his bed!"

"You didn't!" I exclaimed.

"Of course I did! And more than that, I told him that FitzGibbon was in charge of a force of men numbering over five hundred, and I knew it for a fact because I used to supply them with milk and meat ... at least until they stopped paying for it. Not only is FitzGibbon the devil himself, but he doesn't pay his bills! And I told him about the Indians who were all around these parts, and that while I didn't know how many, because they don't buy from me, I figured there must be close to two thousand of them massing and ready . . . ready for an attack on the fort."

FitzGibbon broke into laughter once more, and I couldn't help but join in as well.

"And then, after I'd listened to the men complain and moan, I left behind my butter and walked out with their money in my pocket. Oh, that reminds me," he said as he stood up in his stirrups and dug deep into the front pocket of his pants. "This is for your family," he said, as he reached out to me, dropping coins into my hand. "For your family's butter."

"My Ma said she didn't want any money for the butter."

"I know what she said, and I'm smart enough not to argue with your mother . . . so I'm giving you the coins instead!"

"But—"

"That's an order! Put them away and keep them. You never know when a few coins might come in handy for your family."

That had an ominous tone to it, and it reminded me. Maybe it was time to ask for his help in finding my Pa. I took a deep breath, and swallowed hard.

"I was hoping that you'd be able to help me—"

"Locate your father," FitzGibbon said.

"Yes! How did you know?"

"If it were my father, I would want the same."

I nodded my head. "But there's more," I said softly. "I promised my brother that I wouldn't just find out about him, but that I'd go to my Pa . . . maybe even try to bring him back if I could."

"Bringing him back might not be possible, but I do understand your need to see him. Is the day after tomorrow soon enough for you?"

"Yes, that would be wonderful!" I exclaimed.

"Good. We'll leave the day after tomorrow."

"We? You mean you're coming with me?"

"I have to meet with my commander, and that journey will take me along the road you need to travel. So we'll go together . . . if that's all right with you."

CHAPTER TWELVE

"**W**AKE UP, Tommy."

I sat up. "What's wrong?" It was pitch black and obviously still the middle of the night.

"Nothing is wrong . . . but you have to get up." I recognized the Lieutenant's voice and was both reassured and unnerved. Why did FitzGibbon want me to get up?

"But . . . it's not morning."

"We have to leave right now."

"Leave? Are there Americans coming?" I asked in alarm.

"Nobody is coming. It's time to leave to find your father."

That was right. My Pa. "But why now? I thought we were leaving in the morning," I said, as I crawled to the opening of the tent. Because I was just staying for the night I had bunked down in one of the tents rather than in the DeCews' home.

"Get your pack and kit and meet me by the horses. Be quick . . . and quiet."

FitzGibbon turned and disappeared into the dark while I retreated into the tent to retrieve my things. There were five other men inside and I hoped at least some of them were still asleep. It was difficult in the dark to be certain that I had all my things, but I tried my best to stuff my belongings into my pack. I crawled to the opening again, half carrying, half dragging my pack behind me. I got outside, stood up and then bent over to retie the flap of the tent.

"Tommy . . . good luck . . . and I'm sure he'll be just fine," came Jamison's voice from the tent.

"Thanks," I replied. I finished the last tie and headed for the horses.

A full moon shone down through a cloudless sky and cast enough light to make the steps ahead of me clearly visible. I closed the distance to the horses and could make out at least twenty figures astride their mounts. How many of us were going? Up ahead, well in front of the animals, stood two men. As I approached, I could see that one was FitzGibbon.

"Thomas, this is Captain Ducharme."

"Most pleased to meet you," the other man said with a French accent as he reached out his hand and we shook.

"The Captain and his men are travelling to Burlington Bay and have generously agreed to allow us to accompany them," FitzGibbon explained.

"It is both our pleasure and honour to have your company," Captain Ducharme replied.

"Then we are ready, Captain."

"I'll get my men set while you two take to your mounts." He turned and walked away into the distance to join the column of shadowy figures.

"Come, Tommy, our horses are this way."

Our horses, his big black and my grey, were tethered to a shrub. We untied them and mounted. My horse seemed nervous and fidgety as I settled into the saddle, and I understood how she was feeling.

"Why are we travelling at night?" I asked as I brought my horse up beside the Lieutenant's. I'd done it rarely, and I felt uneasy.

"Best time to travel unobserved."

"Best time to get lost or fall off the edge of a cliff as well," I said.

"Not if you have an Indian guide," FitzGibbon answered.

"Captain Ducharme has an Indian guide?"

FitzGibbon laughed. "All the Captain has is Indian guides. He's in charge of close to two hundred members of the Caughnawaga tribe. Look around," FitzGibbon said, gesturing with a sweep of his arm.

I glanced at the long line of figures in front of us. They were now close enough that I could make out their individual features. In both directions, as far as I could see before the darkness closed in, were Indians! Some were astride their horses while others, in little clusters, stood beside their mounts.

"Don't worry, Tommy. You know not to believe all the stories you've been told," FitzGibbon said quietly.

"I don't . . . I just . . ."

"They're good and honest people. We are going to ride with Captain Ducharme. You can learn much from him about our native allies."

Falling in behind FitzGibbon I moved alongside the column of Indians. I picked up smatterings of muted conversation as I passed—softly spoken and with only an occasional word I could hear, in a language I didn't understand. A few times FitzGibbon called out a greeting to somebody he recognized. One Indian, mounted on his horse, came up beside FitzGibbon and they loudly greeted each other and then clasped hands.

"Tommy, this is somebody I want you to meet!" FitzGibbon announced.

I brought my horse forward.

"This is Tachuck," he said.

The Indian nodded his head at me and I nodded back. He was a large man, and his expression was serious.

"Tachuck and I rode together at the start of the war. I hope we'll all be able to share a meal together some time during the trip."

The hint of a smile broke on Tachuck's face. He nodded his head again, and then moved away. FitzGibbon moved his mount forward and I fell in behind him. We stopped when we reached Captain Ducharme.

The Captain yelled out an order, in words I didn't understand, and the men directly in front of him started into motion along the trail. Behind me, I could hear rustlings as men vanished into the bush on both sides.

"Where are they going?" I asked.

"When we move it isn't just in a thin column of men.

Scouts move throughout the forest . . . like a wave, flowing forward . . . seeing things . . . seeing everything. For us it is safe at the centre of that wave. Come, it is time for us to move."

Ducharme led. FitzGibbon gestured for me to follow, and then he fell in behind me on the narrow path. I soon realized, as we moved along in silence, that this was going to be a long night unbroken by conversation. I settled into the saddle and tried not to think too much.

*   *   *

THE MOONLIGHT had slowly given way to the weak, thin, morning light. I couldn't be certain but I figured we had ridden for almost four hours. All the shadows and shades of grey and black were being replaced by colours, which became more varied and vivid as the day became brighter.

"There's our camp up ahead," Captain Ducharme announced.

I looked past him and saw a small cluster of tents hidden among the trees. I could also see a large fire. Getting closer, I noticed a big pot hanging from a spit above the roaring blaze. But despite the size of the fire there was no smoke rising into the air to mark its existence . . . or our location.

Captain Ducharme dismounted and I did the same. There appeared to be only a half dozen men and horses clustered in the immediate vicinity of the fire. Where were the rest of the Indians?

"Smells like oatmeal," FitzGibbon said.

"It is," Captain Ducharme confirmed. "The Indians say it's the closest thing we have to cornmeal so they have it at least once a day . . . sometimes twice. Personally, I've eaten so much oatmeal I feel as though I'm going to turn into a Scot." He ladled out a bowlful. "Here, have some. Even if you don't like the taste it helps to drive away the night's chill."

I took the bowl. I didn't see any utensils. "Um . . . spoons?"

"You brought what you need with you," the Captain said.

"I did?" I hadn't packed anything like that in my pack. Was I supposed to?

The Captain dipped his fingers into a second bowl of oatmeal and scooped it up into his mouth. "We have to travel light. Just one of the things my Indian brothers have taught me."

"Where are the rest of the Indians?" I asked. I could see no more than a dozen around us.

"There are little clusters and groups spread out all around us."

"Natives are able to just fade into the forest," FitzGibbon explained. "Hundreds of men can be only dozens of feet away but invisible . . . until they want to be seen."

"He's right, Tommy. I've learned a great deal over the past months. Not just how to move through or hide in the forest, but how to live off the land. We require less than a quarter of the food and supplies needed by the regular British soldiers," Captain Ducharme explained.

"What interests me most are the native techniques of warfare," FitzGibbon added.

The Captain agreed. "Those big battles, like two bulls butting their heads together, might work on open plains, but not in the wilds of Canada." He paused. "But look who I'm talking to! You and your Bully Boys use many techniques borrowed from the natives."

"Yes, like taking forest trails instead of roads, using speed and stealth. But I have also heard tales about night fighting."

"Those tales are true. The Indians are very skilled in fighting in the dark of the night," Ducharme confirmed.

FitzGibbon nodded his head. "Is it true that they possess better night vision than whites?"

"The trick, I believe," Ducharme answered, "isn't how well they can see, but instead in knowing where to look. When travelling during the day, the eye of the traveller is most often looking ahead . . . far ahead. Wouldn't you agree?"

FitzGibbon nodded his head.

"At night, you cannot see very far ahead because there is not enough light in the sky."

That seemed pretty obvious, even to me.

"But the traveller who is used to moving only by day, now moving in the dark, still focuses his eyes on the distance, where he can see little. Instead he must be trained to look only slightly ahead . . . a few feet . . . two dozen feet . . . where his eyes *can* see."

"Wouldn't that make it difficult to follow a line, or to know where you're going? You would get lost and—"

"Did we get lost last night as we travelled?" Ducharme asked, interrupting FitzGibbon.

"Of course not, but there was a full moon shining, and—"

"Yes, but the moon was not what guided us. All that was required was the light of the stars. To the natives, the stars in the sky are like signposts on the road."

"So they use the stars the way a sailor uses them to navigate."

"Exactly. They navigate by the stars."

"That all makes sense. Tonight, when we travel, I will try to train my eyes to look no farther than a few dozen feet in front of me," FitzGibbon said.

"But isn't it dangerous not to see what's farther ahead?" I asked. "If you don't see something coming in time how can you prepare for it, or avoid it?"

"That is a danger, Tommy," Captain Ducharme agreed. "But you must remember that when you cannot see hazards, they also cannot see you. During the day you need greater vision, but at night, problems float right by without either side even being aware of the passage."

FitzGibbon let out a laugh. "That is the truth! And when you have two armies speaking the same language, whose militia dress the same, the dark of night can bring both tragic and comic meetings. Up near Niagara there were eight Canadian militiamen who got separated from their company during a battle. They were lost and hungry, but then had the good fortune to wander into the camp of some other militia who were making a meal. They shared conversation and the meal, and then, as they were getting ready to leave, they discovered that these men were Americans! Luckily they left the camp before the enemy discovered who they had invited to dinner!"

Both men started laughing.

"I have a few stories of my own," Captain Ducharme said. "But they'll have to wait until we travel tonight. Right now, I need some sleep. So, good night . . . or should I say, good day, gentlemen."

CHAPTER THIRTEEN

"I DON'T WANT you to get your hopes too high," FitzGibbon said. "This is just one of many places where your father could be."

"I know," I answered softly. I was too tired after another ride through the night to feel much of anything. Maybe that was good.

As soon as we'd arrived at the camp where his commander was stationed, and the Lieutenant had checked in, we were sent to a location where the rest of my Pa's militia company were supposed to be camped. They weren't there, but we found a rear guard unit that was able to direct us to their company. From there, finding that my Pa wasn't with them, we were sent to the area field hospital.

Riding alone with FitzGibbon was different after our two days of travelling with Captain Ducharme and the Caughnawaga warriors. That had been quite an experience. They'd told us stories and showed us some of the ways they did things—ways known to the natives but new to me, and to the Lieutenant as well. I'd even made a friend. He was Tachuck's brother's son, Tuska, and he wasn't much older than me. His English was good enough that we could talk. It turned out that he was one of the natives who summer by the stream not far from our farm. He even invited me to come down sometime to visit him—once all the fighting was over. When I told the Lieutenant about the invitation, he told me how honoured I should be, because the Indians don't usually invite whites into their camp. I guess I was. Maybe he would even come back to my place—that would be something! I couldn't help wondering what my brother and sisters would think about having a real live Indian as a guest! I knew my Ma and Pa wouldn't mind.

Talking to the Indians and learning things had kept my mind occupied and I hadn't had much time to think about my Pa. Now, with it being just the two of us again, I had lots of time to think. That was especially true because we were now safely behind our lines and we could move freely without any worry about American soldiers. Enemy soldiers had been in the back of my mind ever since that day I'd met FitzGibbon in the store.

"That's it up ahead," FitzGibbon said.

At the end of a long lane was a large canvas tent sitting beside a massive red barn. We turned our horses up the lane. Getting closer, I could see the movement of a dozen or more men as they walked between the tent and the barn, while others were simply sitting with their backs against the side of the barn. A few had on the bright-red tunics that identified them as British soldiers, while most were just dressed in regular clothing—militiamen. No one seemed to pay any attention to our arrival, and we dismounted and hitched our horses to a fence.

"You stay by the horses and I'll locate the commander and find out if your father is here." FitzGibbon walked up to one of the soldiers, who pointed toward the tent in answer to his question. FitzGibbon walked over, opened the flap and ducked his head to enter.

I looked around. There were some cows and a dozen horses grazing in the field in the distance. Chickens pecked at the ground nearby for their feed. The fence where we'd tied our horses was one side of a pen, and inside were a couple of dozen hogs, wallowing in the mud. Aside from the large, grey tent and the few men in their uniforms, everything looked peaceful . . . calm . . . normal. This was a fancy farm—certainly not like ours. But I knew that if we kept on working hard, some day our farm could be as fine as this one.

"Tommy!" FitzGibbon called as he came out the door of the tent. He motioned for me to come.

I hurried over. "Is he here?" I asked anxiously.

"He might be. They don't know for sure. We'll have to look."

"Sure," I said, as I went to enter the tent.

FitzGibbon stopped me, putting his hands on my shoulders. "Remember, if he isn't here it doesn't mean anything."

"I know."

"He could be someplace else, or maybe he's even recovered from his wound and has been reassigned to another company."

Or maybe he died from his wound, I thought, but I didn't dare say anything. As long as the words weren't spoken it couldn't be true.

"And Tommy, you have to be prepared. A field hospital is the worst place in any war. Do you understand?"

Although I didn't really know what he meant, I nodded my head. FitzGibbon pulled back the flap of the tent and I entered.

Within two steps I was hit by a wave of foul-smelling air. It was different from anything I'd encountered before. There was a sweet, sickening odour, almost like alcohol, but underneath that was a more powerful smell—like rotting meat.

The tent was crammed full with cots. An aisle was free down the centre, but along both sides were what seemed like hundreds of them, pushed closely together. Each cot was filled with a man, but it would have been easy to overlook them as being nothing more than bedclothing—nobody seemed to be moving. Were they all asleep . . . in the middle of the day?

Part way down the tent a man, trailed by two women, was moving among the patients. As we watched, one of the women came down the aisle toward us. She was carrying a bucket, and as she passed by, we quickly became aware of its contents—the men who were unable to get out of bed had been using it as a toilet. She carried the bucket outside.

We started down the aisle again. I suddenly felt wobbly on my feet. This wasn't what I had expected—not at all. I had to quickly look for my Pa and get back outside.

"Thomas!"

I spun around toward the voice.

"Thomas Roberts, is that you?" a man in one of the beds asked.

"Yes?" I exclaimed, then realizing that it wasn't my father's voice and feeling a rush of disappointment. Who could it be? I walked toward the voice and found a man with the upper part of his head swathed in blood-stained bandages.

"It's so good to see a familiar face," he said softly before erupting into a loud and furious coughing fit.

I had no idea who this man was, but obviously he knew who I was. My goodness, was it really . . . "Mr. Givens?"

"Do I look that bad?" he asked.

"No . . . no . . . it's just that I was surprised." He hardly looked like the man I knew. It wasn't just the bandages covering part of his face. He looked a hundred years older, like he was his own father or grandfather.

"What are you doing so far away from home, Thomas?"

"I'm looking for my Pa," I croaked. "Do you know if he's here?"

He shook his head. "I don't know much. I've lost track of time since I was wounded. I don't even know what day it is. Are you going to be heading back home?"

"Not right away . . . but I will be."

"Could you do a neighbour a favour?" he asked.

"Of course."

"You're a good boy, you are. Can you give something to my wife . . . a letter?"

"Of course I can do that."

"Good. Look under the cot. You'll find my pack, and the letter is right up at the top."

I bent down and reached under the bed, pulling the pack free. I undid the top buckle and pulled out the letter.

"Explain to her that I'm okay. Tell her I'll be home as soon as I can, and apologize to her for me about how messy the writing is. I guess with practice I'll learn to write with my left hand as well as I ever did with my right."

"But why would you—" I stopped myself and a gasp escaped from my lips. Mr. Givens had shifted himself in the bed to reveal the place where his right arm used to be—now gone from the elbow down. The sleeve of his shirt had been cut off and the remaining jagged edge was pinned to his shirt.

He shook his head slowly. "Many are worse than this. At least I'm alive. Just get the letter to my wife."

"I will, Mr. Givens . . . it might take me a few weeks, but I'll do it," I said, the words escaping as a whisper. "I have to go . . . I have to find my Pa."

"Thank you, Thomas!" he called out after me as I staggered down the aisle and away from him.

"Tommy," FitzGibbon said as he reached out and grabbed me firmly by the shoulder, stopping me. "You can't rush by anybody. You have to look at each man, carefully. Your father might have his face bandaged, or he might be asleep and turned away from you, or he could look—"

"Different than I remember him," I said, completing his sentence. I'd passed right by Mr. Givens, a man I'd known my whole life. If he hadn't called out to me I would never have seen him. What if my Pa was asleep when I passed, or too sick or feverish to see me and couldn't call out to me? I needed to look in the face of every man here . . . every single man.

*   *   *

I PUSHED out through the flap of the tent and into the bright sunlight and fresh air. When I slumped to the ground the cool, slightly damp ground felt refreshing. I inhaled deeply, taking in the smell of the earth and the grass—hoping it would overpower the stench of the hospital tent that still lingered in my nostrils.

It had been hard, maybe the hardest thing I'd ever done in my life, but I'd looked at each man—looked hard at them, even when I wanted to turn away or run. Some had stopped me, even reached out to grab me by the hand. They wanted to talk—needed to talk. And I guess I needed to talk to them as well, just to make sure. Two other wounded men were neighbours I knew. One had been asleep—at least I hoped he was just sleep—and I passed by without him even being aware I had ever been there. The second man, a relative of the Watson family, had greeted me with a hearty hello. His wounds weren't serious and he was eager to rejoin his company. He hadn't seen or heard of my Pa either, which made me think we were wasting our time at this hospital.

Slowly, carefully, I looked at each man, certain that none of them was my Pa. And I now knew he wasn't in there. He wasn't one of the hundred or so men, lying in bed. Some seemed fine, but most were unmoving, eyes closed. Others had their eyes open but stared unseeing into space. But most disturbing were those who sobbed or quietly moaned, with nobody to hear their cries of pain or anguish. My Pa wasn't there . . . but where was he?

FitzGibbon came out of the tent and sat down on the grass beside me. I heard him take a deep breath, and I saw in his expression that he was upset.

"You never get used to this part . . . at least I never do," he said, looking over at me. "Are you all right?"

"I guess so . . . I just need some air."

"I don't know which is worse, the smell or the sight. I imagine you've not seen much of wounded soldiers before."

I shook my head. "Just the few who were wounded when the blockhouse was stormed." My mind raced back to that dead American that I'd stumbled over as I walked through the gate. He was the only dead man I had seen.

"I remember my first campaign, that very first battle, and then seeing the wounded men. We're much more ingenious in devising ways to harm or kill our fellow man than we are in our ability to heal."

"We do our best," called out a voice.

We turned around. It was the doctor.

"I didn't mean any offence," FitzGibbon apologized.

"I'm sure you didn't." He sat down on the grass beside us. "Maybe I should apologize to you. I haven't had more than a few hours' sleep at a time for the past three weeks. My wife says I get cranky if I don't have enough rest. And I guess there's no denying what you said about the ingenuity of man to kill and maim his fellow man. I look at some of these men and I know I can't do anything." He shook his head. "But the worst are those whom I could help if I had the time and tools available. Do you know how many limbs I've removed because I didn't have the time to try and save them?"

I wondered if Mr. Givens was one of those . . . or maybe my Pa.

"How many were wounded in the battle?" I asked.

"I don't know the exact number. My hands were full with the skirmishes before the battle, and then wounded kept pouring in for days after. I know I've tended to over two hundred men."

"By yourself?" I asked in amazement.

"With the help of my two nurses. Poor women have slept even less than me. Angels is what they are, blessed angels of mercy. So you didn't find your father," the doctor said.

I shook my head. "He wasn't in the tent."

"And not in the barn either?" he asked.

"I didn't know there were any wounded in the barn."

"There wasn't room in the tent for all of the men so I had to move many into the barn. To tell you the truth, I think it's cleaner and better than the tent anyway. Go on in there and have a look. If you don't locate him then you come back to me and I'll be able to direct you to the other two field hospitals."

"We appreciate that, Doctor," FitzGibbon said.

"It's the least I can do. I'm just sorry that I wasn't able to give you more information. I know that each man is somebody's father or husband or son, but . . . I'm too busy trying to save lives to keep track of whose life I've been saving." The doctor stood up. "I think I've been away too long now . . . I'd better get back." He took a deep breath. "This job makes you appreciate the wondrous smell of fresh air. Good day, gentlemen . . . and may luck be with you." He walked away and disappeared back into the tent.

FitzGibbon and I sat in silence for awhile. I was thinking about the adventure of battle, about the camaraderie of soldiers that I'd so much envied when I first met the Bully Boys. I'd imagined my father and uncle sitting by a cook fire listening to talks of glory—but I'd never imagined this.

"Well, Tommy, are you ready to have a look in the barn now?"

"Maybe . . . do you think we could just sit here for a couple more minutes before we go into—"

"Tommy!"

I looked up. It was Pa!

CHAPTER FOURTEEN

"P**A!**" I screamed as I ran to him. I threw my arms around my father and tried to stop myself from breaking into tears. I knew they weren't far away.

"Gently, Tommy . . . gently. You practically knocked me over."

"I didn't mean to." I released my grip and stepped slightly back. "You're all right?" I said. It was as much a question as it was a comment and a hope. I choked back the tears.

"Of course I'm all right."

I looked at him hard. His voice was low and soft and

his face looked pale and gaunt. He was also leaning on a cane.

"But you were wounded . . ."

He laughed—not his usual laugh, but a hollow, raspy version. "Wounded twice. One shot nicked my side. Right where you were squeezing me."

"I'm so sorry! I didn't mean to—"

"That's okay, you didn't know. And the second musket ball hit me in the leg."

"Your leg! But they didn't have to . . ." I was thinking about Mr. Givens's arm.

"No, Tommy, I still have my leg," he said as he reached down and pulled up the cuff of his pants. "See? The shot hit it farther up. Went in one side and out the other. I'll need this cane for a while, but I'll be fine." He paused and his brow furrowed. "But why are you here? Has something happened?"

"Everybody, everything is fine, Pa . . . honest. It's just, we got a message, from Mr. McGregor, about you being wounded . . ."

His face twisted into a grimace. "I'm sure he was trying to be helpful, but I didn't want any of you to know anything about it. I didn't want to worry you none."

"We didn't know how bad you were hurt. That's why I had to come."

"You all must have been worried sick, especially your mother. You know she worries about everything." His face took on a serious look. "It wasn't safe for you to come all this way across country and through enemy lines."

"I was fine. It wasn't like I was alone."

"Who came with you . . . not your brother."

"He wanted to come, but I made him stay on the farm. I came with Captain Ducharme and close to two hundred Caughnawaga braves, and of course Lieutenant FitzGibbon."

"FitzGibbon . . . James FitzGibbon, the leader of the Bully Boys?"

"At your service, sir." FitzGibbon had been hanging back, but now he stepped forward and they shook hands. I could tell from my Pa's expression he was stunned. Even more stunned and surprised than when he had seen me.

"*You* brought my son here?" he asked in disbelief.

"I had to report to the area commander, and I knew how concerned Tommy and your whole family were about your well-being, and as I'm greatly in your son's debt, I—"

"But how did you know of my family's concern?"

"Well . . ." FitzGibbon began. I was sure he was debating what parts to tell and what parts to keep quiet about for now.

I jumped in. In one long sentence I explained how I came to meet the Lieutenant, and how I was helping out at the DeCew farm. I was careful not to mention anything else. My Pa wasn't the only one who didn't want to worry people.

"My good Lord," my Pa said when I finished. "I'm proud of you, Tommy. But your mother—how is she getting along? Is Johnny doing all the farmwork now? There aren't enough hours in the day for one man, let alone one boy, to get in all the crops we'll need . . . the crops the family will need to live through the winter."

I explained about the bags of flour I'd earned working at the DeCews' and how I'd brought the food to the family. My Pa put a hand on my shoulder and the look on his face told me how proud he was—prouder I thought than he'd looked after hearing about me saving the Lieutenant.

"Will my son return under your protection as well, Lieutenant?" my Pa asked.

"I will guarantee his safe return. It is a pleasure to travel in his company. He is a fine young man."

"He is that," my Pa said.

I looked down at the ground. I felt myself turning red and hoped I was the only one to notice.

"How long can he stay with me, Lieutenant?"

"My duties call for me to be elsewhere for a day. I could pass back this way tomorrow. Would he have a place to stay here overnight?"

"Certainly!"

"In the tent?" I asked anxiously.

"Out in the barn with me." He paused. "I wouldn't have you stay at all if you had to be lodged in the tent for the night."

"Then I will take leave and let you spend time with your son. Good day, gentlemen."

"It was an honour to meet you, Lieutenant. And while you may be in the debt of my son, I am equally in yours. Thank you."

They shook hands once again and FitzGibbon walked off. We watched as he climbed onto his horse, waved and trotted off. My father wrapped an arm around my shoulder. It felt good.

"Are you hungry?" Pa asked.

"Yeah, sure!"

"It's good that at least one thing about you hasn't changed. Come on and I'll get you some grub."

"Could that wait a couple of minutes? I have to take care of my horse."

"You didn't take Bessy, did you?"

Bessy was our plough horse. "No sir. I have my own horse."

"Your own horse! Where did you go getting yourself a horse?"

"Well, it's sort of my animal. The Lieutenant says it's mine. It belonged to the American soldier, the one I hit on the head. I always ride it. She's right over there," I said, pointing to my grey tethered to a fence.

"Fine-looking horse. I'll show you where to feed and water her. With the wounded taking the barn, all the animals are being kept out in the back pen."

My Pa took a few steps, leaning heavily on his cane. I was shocked by the awkwardness of his gait, and I could see that he was fighting against showing me the pain he was feeling. He knew full well that I was watching.

"It isn't as bad as it looks," he said.

I slowed down my pace to match his stride. Reaching the fence, he gave my grey horse a rub behind the ears.

"Good lines, strong, solid legs," he said. "Might make a good plough horse."

"Maybe," I said, although I'd never thought of her

being used that way. She was an army horse, meant for battle. "Is it far to the pens?"

"Just around the back of the barn. Not far."

Not far for me, but plenty far for my Pa, I thought. There were beads of sweat on his forehead that had nothing to do with the weather but everything to do with the strain of walking even this short distance.

"Do you want to ride her?" I asked, hoping to get him off his feet. "See what a good mount she is?"

"She's your horse, Tommy. You're the only one who should ride her." He paused and looked directly into my eyes. "I can walk, Tommy."

"But it would be easier for me to—"

"Don't go arguing with your Pa. I may not have a switch handy but I'm still man enough to give your backside a swat with this here cane."

"Yes sir," I said. I climbed up on my horse. Pa started walking, slowly, limping away, and I followed, reining in the horse to try to walk at as slow a pace as he did. I looked down at him as we moved—me sitting effortlessly in the saddle and him struggling and straining to earn every foot of ground. I trailed behind as we circled around the barn and started up a slope that led to the back of the building. There was a large fenced pen and more than two dozen horses moved inside. Pa stopped.

"Here we are."

I climbed off, quickly unbuckled the saddle, pulled it off and propped it over the top rail of the fence where some other saddles were sitting. I slipped the gate open, led the grey inside and closed the gate after us. Next I removed the bridle and reins. There was a full trough of water and a couple of bales of hay broken open in the pen.

"There you go, girl," I said as I gave her a gentle tap on the side. She trotted off and went straight to the water.

"So where is that food you were talking—" I stopped short. Pa looked as white as a sheet and was leaning heavily against the top rail of the fence, like it was the only thing keeping him from tumbling right down. I rushed over, scared and breathless, and my head was filled with a terrible scramble of ideas. Had I found him, just to watch him die?

"Pa!" I held onto his arm. He leaned over even more and I strained unsuccessfully to keep him up. He slumped down to the ground.

"I'm okay . . . just a little weak . . . I guess I pushed too hard." He took a deep breath. Sweat was just pouring off his face.

"Do you want me to go and get the doctor?"

He shook his head. "He's got more important things, more badly hurt men to tend to. People worse off than me. There's nothing more he can do anyway. He just tells me to rest . . . so let me rest for a while." He closed his eyes and took a number of deep breaths. "I was a fool to push myself like this. My pride got in the way of my common sense. But it's like the Good Book says, pride goes before a fall. Or in this case, pride went before a seat on the grass."

He smiled and I smiled back. He was all right. I sat down on the grass beside him and watched him out of the corner of my eye, so he couldn't tell I was looking. He'd lost some weight—not as much as Mr. Givens, but he was definitely thinner. And I was sure that he was shaking as he sat there beside me.

"It's a shame about Mr. Givens," I said.

"Yeah, it is. He's going to have some trouble taking care of his farm. But he's a stubborn man, and I imagine he'll get by."

"It'll be hard," I said.

"You know that's probably the thing men fear almost as much as death . . . being cut up like that . . . losing an arm or a leg."

I didn't know what to say so I just stayed silent.

"There's things I've seen and heard that I'll never forget as long as I live. Sights and sounds and even smells of the battlefield. Awful . . ."

I shuddered.

"But there is one thing even worse."

"What?" I couldn't imagine.

"Dying on the field of battle and then being denied a Christian burial, your family never knowing what happened in the end."

"That would never happen!"

"Sometimes there are just so many bodies that there isn't time. Something has to be done before they start to spread disease. Disease has killed more soldiers than bullets. You can't let concern for the dead be more important than the fate of the living. That's one of the prices of losing a battle," he continued. "The enemy takes over the ground where the battle took place and then has to dispose of the corpses. Usually they're too busy caring for their own people to worry much for the remains of the enemy. They put them to the flame as soon as they can."

"What do you mean?"

"They toss the bodies onto a gigantic fire. All that's left is ashes . . . nothing more . . . nothing to say who once was." Pa got a far away look in his eyes. "Nothing left." He shook his head and then turned to me.

Again I didn't know what to say, but I'd certainly lost some of my appetite.

"There's so much of this I wish I could change, Thomas."

It was always serious when he called me by my full name.

"I know you wanted to come with me and your uncle. Be part of things. And I guess if I was your age I would have felt the same. But it isn't some game."

"I know that, Pa."

"I was hoping you did. I wish I had no part of this war."

"You mean you didn't want to fight?" I asked. I couldn't imagine my father ever backing away from a fight.

He shook his head. "What man in his right mind would want to be part of killing or being killed? I only fought because we had no choice." He paused. "I had no quarrel with the Americans . . . at least not until they invaded our country."

We sat silently side by side. I wasn't sure if he was thinking or just needed more time to rest. When he spoke again, there was a fierceness in his words.

"I want you back on the farm as soon as you can get there. Working the fields and staying as far away from all this as you can. Understand?"

"Yes, sir."

I wasn't about to say no to my Pa, and I understood what he was trying to say, but I had to wonder if the chance came for me to fight—maybe even with FitzGibbon and his men—would I be able to obey my father's wishes?

"Now let's go and get some food." He started to get up.

"Are you sure you're okay?"

"I'm fine. I've got to get up and walk. Got to." He pulled himself to his feet, and I stood up beside him. I wanted to take his arm or help him, but I knew I couldn't. The best I could manage was to stay close enough to catch him if he fell again.

"And do you know why I have to walk?"

"No sir."

"Because if I can walk again, then I can farm again, and if I can farm I can provide for my family, and I have to provide. No matter what, I have to take care of my family. That's the only reason I'm part of this war . . . to take care of my family. Do you understand, Tommy? Do you?"

I nodded my head. "I understand completely," I answered truthfully. I knew exactly what he meant. A few short weeks ago, I didn't think I would have.

* * *

"AND THEN I'm planning on deserting and joining the American forces."

"What did you say?" I exclaimed, turning in my saddle to face FitzGibbon.

"Oh, good, I thought you had fallen asleep in the saddle."

"But you said you were going to—"

FitzGibbon laughed. "I was just trying to get your attention. You haven't been responding to anything I've said for the last three hours. Being just the two of us on this ride has made for poor conversation."

"I was just . . . just thinking," I admitted.

"I hoped you were just lost in thought and hadn't passed away." He paused. "Your father is going to be fine."

Of course FitzGibbon was right about what was occupying my mind. I couldn't stop thinking about my Pa. I just hoped he was also right about Pa getting better. "Do you really think so?"

"Of course I do. Tommy, you know me well enough to know that I never lie . . . well, except when I'm dealing with the Americans. I've seen enough men wounded in battle and I know that it's the first few days that are the most critical. After that they don't die from the wound, but from the infection or disease that sets in. Your father's wound is healing well, he's getting stronger."

"I guess you're right," I admitted. He had been stronger the second day, and from what he had told me he was already much, much stronger than he had been the week before.

"And it's not just my opinion."

"What do you mean?"

"I spoke to the doctor on behalf of you and your mother. He said that your father is making a good recovery."

"So he'll be able to walk again . . . be as good as before?"

"I didn't say that."

I knew it, but I was hoping that by saying it I could make it come true.

"There's no way of knowing, although I would suspect, if he's like his son, he'll overcome this. Is he a stubborn man?"

I laughed. "My Ma says he's the second most stubborn person in the entire world . . . after her."

"Then he'll do well. What we have to arrange is to get word to your mother. To let her and your family know that he's going to be fine, and to tell them when he's going to be coming home."

"Coming home? He's coming home?" I exclaimed.

FitzGibbon smiled and nodded his head. "I spoke to both the doctor *and* the area commander, Colonel Breckon. The war is over for your father. His wounds will require rest and time. As soon as he's able he'll be moved back across the American lines to your farm. His recovery and health will be better served among his family. He doesn't need a doctor any more. What he needs is rest, food and the love of his family."

"When will he be going home?" I asked excitedly.

"A few weeks, perhaps a month, it depends on where the fighting is taking place and whether they can find a safe way through enemy lines."

"That's . . . that's . . . thank you," I said.

"Why are you thanking me?" FitzGibbon asked. "I'm nothing more than the bearer of the good news. I did nothing but—"

FitzGibbon stopped mid-sentence as we both heard the neighing of a horse.

"How far are we from the American lines?" I asked quietly.

"We passed into American territory about thirty minutes ago. Let's dismount and have a look."

FitzGibbon jumped off his horse and I did the same. We walked the horses off the trail and into some bushes, looping our reins lightly over a branch. By now I knew not to tie the horses in case we had to leave quickly: the difference between simply jumping on a horse and riding away instead of having to first untie it could be the difference between life and death.

FitzGibbon slipped his rifle off of the horse's saddle and I did the same. Crouched over, he headed back toward the path and I followed. I was painfully aware of the sound of a twig snapping under my foot as we moved forward. We stopped right beside the path and hid behind some thick bushes amid a smattering of small trees and saplings.

"Do you see anything?" I whispered.

"Nothing. You?"

"Nothing. Maybe it just sounded like a horse," I said hopefully.

"It was a horse, but there's no telling how far away it was. It could even have been one of our men, or maybe even a stray horse that lost its rider."

"So what do we do now?" I asked.

"The hardest thing a soldier has to do. Wait. Keep your ears and eyes open. I'm just going to—"

There was an explosion of musket fire and I ducked as I heard a shot whistle by my ear. I turned to FitzGibbon. He had toppled over backwards and lay on the ground, unmoving, a crumpled heap. I froze in fear.

CHAPTER FIFTEEN

H E WAS SHOT! He wasn't moving. Was he? The sound of another shot exploded and I jumped off to the side. I saw the puff of smoke rise into the air to signal the location of the shooters. There were three of them, in bright-blue American uniforms, huddled close together. Two were frantically reloading their muskets and the third, who had just fired the last shot, started to do the same. I had to run . . . get away before any of them had time to reload . . . I had only seconds to escape! But what about FitzGibbon? I couldn't just leave him there. There was only one thing to do.

I brought my rifle up to my eye. I sighted the first man, the one who had just shot, and then changed my mind—he wouldn't be able to shoot at me for another thirty seconds. I aimed for one of the others. One of the men had finished reloading his weapon and was training his gun in my direction, getting ready to fire. I knew I had an advantage, because my rifle was much more accurate than his musket. Calmly I sighted his chest and fired. A split second after the recoil of the weapon against my shoulder and the explosion of the shot, I saw him thrown backwards. I'd hit him!

The second American aimed his musket and I threw myself to the ground just an instant before I heard the retort of his gun. Just off to the side was FitzGibbon's rifle. I rolled over, grabbed it and brought it up, ready to shoot. The third American had now reloaded while the other still standing started reloading again. I steadied the rifle against a fallen tree and aimed squarely at the chest of the soldier ready to fire. Was he the one who had killed FitzGibbon? I shot and he fell to the ground!

The third American, the only one left, jumped back in panic at the sight of the second soldier falling, and his musket fell to the side. He scrambled to pick it up. He hadn't finished loading. I could get away now. Or maybe he'd run . . . run to get more men. There was another choice: Could I get to him before he had a chance to reload?

"AAAAAAAAAHHHH!" I screamed as I jumped over the fallen log and ran toward him. I closed the short gap between us, smashing through the bushes and saplings, the branches stinging as they snapped against my face. He struggled to get the charge in the gun, fumbled it, and again the musket fell to the ground. He looked up at me and then ran, leaving his weapon behind. He vanished into the thick underbrush and I knew there was no way I could catch him. And what would I have done if I had? That thought left me stunned. My rifle wasn't even loaded. Was I planning to catch him and kill him with my bare hands? The only thing more shocking than that thought was the realization that if he had stopped and stood his ground I would certainly have killed him . . . unless he'd killed me first.

I stopped, right at the point where he'd been struggling to reload. My heart was pounding and every part of my body tingled. Was it from fear or excitement? I picked up his weapon and turned to start back. I had to go to the Lieutenant. Maybe he was still alive. I could get him onto his horse and get him back to the field hospital. It was only four or five hours away and—

I heard a low groan. I spun around toward the sound. I didn't see anything.

I trained the rifle all around, looking. My eyes stopped momentarily on the one American soldier. He lay on his front, face down, a gaping hole exposed in the middle of his back—the place where a bullet, *my* bullet, had passed out of his body.

I heard a louder groan, followed by the sound of vomiting, and I spun to the side. It was the other American. He was propped up on one elbow. His eyes were closed. I froze, my rifle pointing at him.

Then his eyes opened, and he was staring directly at me. He pushed himself up so he was almost in a sitting position. I thought about pulling the trigger, shooting him, killing him. Taking revenge for what he had done to FitzGibbon and to my Pa and Mr. Givens . . . but the gun wasn't loaded. I slowly lowered the rifle and looked at him, but not through the sights of the weapon. He was harmless, lying there, bleeding. He was no threat to me. If the gun had been loaded, though, could I at that second have stopped myself from pulling the trigger? A shudder ran through my entire body.

There was a growing patch of red staining the blue of his uniform which was tattered and torn around his left shoulder, the place where the rifle shot had entered his body. His musket lay just off to the side. Had he loaded it before he was shot? Would he reach out now and get it when I turned my back to leave? I had no choice. I had to go closer and take his weapon or at least move it farther away from him so he couldn't use it against me.

Still holding my rifle in front of me, like a shield, I moved forward. He had moved slightly so his back was now propped against a small tree. His eyes were closed. Was he dead? I inched toward him, stopped, bent over and reached out to take his weapon from the ground.

"Was it you?"

I jumped back, his musket in my hand. He was looking at me.

"Was it you?" he rasped softly. "Was it you who shot me?"

Numbly I nodded my head.

"And my friend, Samuel . . . is he dead?" he asked, gesturing to the other fallen soldier.

Again I nodded. "I think so."

"How old are you, son?"

"Fourteen, sir," I said.

He coughed loudly, and his whole body suddenly

shuddered, his face contorted in pain. "I have a son who will be thirteen on his next birthday . . . in October . . ."

His body started to shake violently and he threw up again. Bright yellow bile dripped from the edges of his mouth.

"What's . . . what's your name?" he asked haltingly.

I hesitated.

"I have the right to know . . . the name of the man who . . . who killed me."

"You're not . . . you're not . . ."

He coughed loudly and I could see the pain on his face. The stain of blood on his uniform seemed much larger now. "I'm dead . . . I know that. Tell me your name."

"It's Tommy, um, Thomas, Thomas Roberts."

"Thomas Roberts, will you do me a favour?"

"What sort of favour?"

He motioned with his hand for me to come closer. I froze in place.

"Don't be afraid, Thomas . . . you have nothing to fear from me . . . not now."

I stepped forward and bent down.

Slowly and with great effort he used his good hand to reach into a pocket. He pulled out an envelope. "Make sure this gets to my wife," he said in a whisper as he pressed it into my hand. "Her name . . . our farm . . . it's all there on the envelope. Can you do that, Thomas?"

I nodded my head dumbly. This was the second letter I'd been given to deliver.

"Good man. And can you tell her . . . maybe write it down . . . do you write, Thomas?"

"Yes, sir."

"Write her. Tell her I died in battle . . . and tell her . . . tell her and tell . . . my children . . . that I loved them. Can you do that, Thomas?"

"Yes, sir."

"Thank you, Thomas. Now go . . . quickly. There's more of us not far from here and they'll be back soon. Go . . . there's been enough death today."

I clutched the letter tightly in my hand, turned and started away. I stumbled, tripped, almost fell over, regained my balance and stumbled again. My feet felt like lead . . . I couldn't seem to pick them up. I had to get away. I couldn't be there when he died.

I had to find FitzGibbon. My head was spinning and I couldn't tell one direction from the other. Where were the horses? I had to find them. I had to think . . . calm down . . . think this through . . . not panic. All at once my stomach churned violently and I threw up. I dropped to my knees as my stomach heaved again. My eyes blurred and I was afraid I was going to pass out. This was like some sort of terrible nightmare. What was I going to do? I brought a hand up and rubbed my eyes. And then I saw FitzGibbon . . . sitting with his back against a tree, rubbing his chest!

CHAPTER SIXTEEN

"LIEUTENANT!" I screamed. He was alive! Suddenly as light as a feather I bounded over fallen trees and crashed through bushes to get to his side.

"You're alive!"

"Very," he said, in a weak voice. Both hands were holding his chest. He took a deep breath, his chest rose, and he winced in pain. "And the Americans?"

"One's dead and another's badly wounded."

"Were there only two of them?" FitzGibbon asked.

"No, sir. There was a third. He ran off."

"Hopefully he'll have to travel some distance to get help."

"No, there are other Americans close by," I said.

"You've seen them?" he asked in alarm.

"No . . . but the wounded man . . . he told me."

"You spoke to him?"

"Yes."

"And he asked me to give this to his wife," I said, showing him the letter I still clutched in my hand.

"Is he badly hurt?"

"The shot hit him in the chest. He's bleeding . . . a lot. He said I should get out of here before they come back."

"He's right. Let's get to the horses." FitzGibbon struggled to his feet. He staggered and I grabbed him by the arm to help him stay up.

"Where were you hit?" I asked anxiously. I couldn't see any blood flowing or wound visible on his chest, beneath his hand.

"Right here," he said, moving his hands to reveal the spot on his chest that he'd been clutching.

"But . . . but . . . there's no . . ."

"No, no wound, but here's what hit me." he said. He held out a flattened piece of metal and dropped it into my hand. "A musket ball. They flatten when they hit."

I stood there in wide-eyed, open-mouthed amazement. "It flattened when it hit you?" That couldn't be possible.

"*Before* it hit me. You see that sapling?" he said, pointing to a small tree that had been snapped off about four and a half feet above the ground.

I nodded.

"I think the ball went right through that tree. It cut the top off as it passed through, but the tree slowed the bullet down, flattened it out, and then it hit me . . . right here," FitzGibbon said.

He pulled out the picture of his fiancée from his pocket. The glass had been shattered and the picture itself looked as though it had been burned.

"The leather behind the picture absorbed the last energy of the shot."

"Then you're not hurt!"

"I didn't say that. I feel like I've been kicked in the chest by a mule. The force of the blow knocked me backwards and unconscious, but it didn't even break the skin." He paused and tried to take a deep breath, grimacing in pain. "The Americans might be back at any second. Let's get to the horses." He looked around on the ground. "Where's my rifle?"

"I had to borrow it. I dropped it back there," I said,

pointing back across the field to where I'd dropped to my knees and vomited. Somehow the letter had remained firmly gripped in my hand even when I let go of both FitzGibbon's rifle and the American's musket.

"And yours?"

"I dropped it after I shot. It's over there somewhere," I said, motioning to the thick underbrush. "I'll go and look for it."

FitzGibbon grabbed me by the arm. "We don't have time. We have to get to the horses. It's that way," he said.

I took off like a shot, but FitzGibbon wasn't with me. I turned around and saw that he had stopped and was bent over. I hurried back to his side.

"Are you sure you're all right?"

He nodded his head. "Just having trouble . . . getting my breath," he panted. "Can you bring the horses here?"

Pushing through a thick stand of brush I was relieved to see the horses. I grabbed the reins, and started to pull them back. My mount came willingly, but FitzGibbon's was reluctant to follow and I had to give a solid tug to get him to comply. Getting closer I saw that FitzGibbon was now sitting. His mouth was open and he was holding his chest. He stood at my approach, again staggering and almost falling back to the ground.

"Thanks," FitzGibbon said as he took the reins of his horse. He placed his foot in the stirrups and with great effort hoisted himself up. I leaped onto my grey.

"Are we heading back to the field hospital?" I asked.

"Of course not. We must go to our camp."

"But what about your chest? You need to be looked at by the doctor!"

"There's nothing that he can do."

"What do you mean?" I asked.

"All that he will be able to say is that I'm banged up inside." He paused and took another deep breath. "Maybe I just need to rest and it will heal by itself, or maybe something inside is hurt badly . . . if that's the case there's nothing he can do anyway."

His face was now deathly pale. "Maybe it would be better if I don't talk for a while."

"You not talk?"

FitzGibbon laughed and then grimaced. "And maybe not laugh, either."

CHAPTER SEVENTEEN

OW ARE you doing today, Tommy?" FitzGibbon asked as I emerged from my tent.

"I'm fine," I answered. Fine, but with hardly a wink of sleep the last night . . . or the night before. "How are *you*?"

"Everybody's been very interested in my health these last few days," FitzGibbon answered.

"And what are you answering today?"

He smiled. "I'm better than I was yesterday, but not as good as I'm planning on being tomorrow. I was just speaking to Matthew Williams."

Matthew had been sent to tell my family all about my Pa. "Did he speak to my Ma?"

FitzGibbon nodded. "He even dropped off that letter from Mr. Givens on the way to your farm. He told me your family was so happy about your father that they wouldn't let him leave without sharing a meal with him. He said it was a feast!"

"My Ma says food makes good news better, and bad news easier to swallow." I would have liked to have been there. It wasn't just my family I missed but my Ma's cooking. There was always plenty of food in camp but it seemed that nothing tasted quite as good when they had to cook enough of it to feed fifty or more men.

We were back at the DeCews' farm. FitzGibbon's Bully Boys were once again making their camp there. And I was back at work for Mr. DeCew, this time at the mill.

"I'm feeling so well I'm thinking of taking a little ride today," FitzGibbon said. "Are you interested in coming along?"

"Where would we be going to?" I asked hesitantly.

"Not near the front . . . just into the countryside. I want to make sure I'm as well as I think I am. A good hard ride will let me know if I've healed sufficiently to get back into action."

"I'd like to come along . . . if Mr. DeCew can spare me."

"He says you've worked so hard the last two days you deserve a day off."

I *had* been working hard. Hard work seemed like the best thing to keep my mind occupied.

FitzGibbon walked away a few steps and took a seat, his back resting against a tree. He motioned for me to join him and I slumped down on the grass.

"Have you been thinking about the men you felled in battle?"

I nodded.

"You know, you're not supposed to just forget about it."

There was no danger of me ever forgetting about it. It was like FitzGibbon had said to me the first time he'd passed me a rifle—when you shoot a man it changes you forever. At the time I hadn't really understood. Now I did. I had changed.

Whenever I was alone I heard the man's voice, and when I closed my eyes at night I saw his face. Thank goodness the other man's face had been turned to the ground. I couldn't bear the thought of having more than one set of eyes haunting me when I closed mine.

"I remember the first man I killed. I was older than you, nearly twenty-two, fighting in Europe against Napoleon. I shot and I saw him fall, and then I was swept away in the heat of battle," FitzGibbon said.

"How did you know you'd killed him?"

"When the fighting ended I was one of those assigned to bury the bodies. I helped put him in the ground," he said quietly.

"So you didn't talk to him."

FitzGibbon shook his head. "He was dead. Long dead. I didn't even know his name." FitzGibbon paused. "And I certainly wasn't asked to deliver a letter to his wife."

The letter was in my breast pocket. I'd thought about how I could get it to the man's wife—I knew it couldn't possibly happen until the war ended. I imagined what it would be like to hand it to her myself . . . to see her, and the children of the man I'd killed. Next to it was the letter I'd started to write, the letter to explain what had happened to him. I'd only written the first line . . . I barely knew what to say.

"I know it's hard, Tommy, but you have to remember not just what you did, but why you did it."

I nodded.

"You did what was necessary. You didn't take those

men's lives by choice, but because you had no alternative. If you hadn't shot them they would have killed both of us. You were merely a soldier doing what he needed to do and—"

"Lieutenant!" shouted a soldier as he came running up.

"What is it?"

"A woman was just brought in by some of Captain Ducharme's Caughnawagas. She's demanding to talk to you!"

"Is she from around these parts?" FitzGibbon asked.

"No sir, she said she's from Queenston."

My ears perked up at the mention of the village I knew better than any other place in the world. Who could it be?

"It must be important. That's a long ride," FitzGibbon said.

"She didn't ride . . . she walked."

"From Queenston? That's over twenty miles!" FitzGibbon said in amazement.

"That's what she said, sir."

"Where is she?"

"She's up at the DeCews' home."

FitzGibbon turned to me. "You must know practically everybody who lives in Queenston."

"Everybody."

"Good. Come along with me."

I gladly trailed behind the Lieutenant as he hurried up to the farmhouse. He pulled open the kitchen door, holding it for me, and I entered ahead of him. Mrs. DeCew was standing beside a woman who was sitting at the table. The woman's back was to me, but she turned around as she heard us enter.

"Thomas!" she cried as she stood up and came toward me.

Of course I recognized her instantly. It was Mrs. Secord. She and her husband and children, one of whom had been in the same form as me in school, lived just on the edge of town, not more than a ten-minute walk from our farm.

"Mrs. Secord, what are you doing here?"

"I had to come and give warning!" she exclaimed.

Her hair was wild and unkempt. There were smudges of dirt on her face, and I noticed her dress was both muddy and torn along the bottom.

"I have to speak to Lieutenant FitzGibbon!" she continued.

"At your service," the Lieutenant said as he nodded his head.

"Thank goodness I've found you! You have to leave!"

"Leave? But I just got here," he said playfully.

"No, no, you don't understand, you have to leave here! You and your men! The Americans are plotting to capture you!"

"The Americans are always trying to capture me," he said matter-of-factly.

"But they have a plan . . . they're coming *here*," she said.

"Here?" He shook his head. "The Americans never venture this far afield. Besides, how would they even know where to look?"

"I overheard the Americans making their plans. That's how *I* knew where to look," she said.

FitzGibbon nodded solemnly. Certainly what she had said made perfect sense.

"Mrs. Secord, I want you to sit down, have a sip of that tea that Mrs. DeCew has just set down at the table, and I'll join you."

"Certainly . . . I would love a cup of tea . . . I haven't had more than a mouthful of water or food since first light yesterday morning."

She went to sit down and FitzGibbon turned around to the two soldiers who were standing by the door. "Ask

Captain Ducharme to send out scouting parties of Indians, especially along the routes to Fort George," he said quietly. "And I want pickets to be doubled, with a second set stationed farther afield."

"Yes, sir," one soldier responded, and they both headed out the door.

"Mrs. DeCew, could you bring two more cups—one for myself and a second for Tommy? And I think all three of us would be most grateful for a small plate of your wonderful bread and marmalade as well."

Mrs. DeCew smiled and turned to get the food while the two of us took seats at the table beside Mrs. Secord.

"So tell me, Mrs. Secord, how is it that you came to know of the plans of the Americans?"

"I overheard them. In my home, over dinner. There were four of them talking about their plans. How they were going to come here to this farm and capture or kill you, Lieutenant FitzGibbon."

"You had American soldiers as your dinner guests?" I asked in amazement. I'd heard of settlers betraying the Crown and aiding the Americans, but I would never have suspected the Secords.

"Oh, goodness no!" Mrs. Secord exclaimed. "They were far from my guests! We were forced to take in

American soldiers . . . feed them . . . let them use our homes for a few days as though it were some sort of hotel and we were their servants!"

"How terrible to have to entertain the enemy," FitzGibbon said.

"And after what they did to my husband . . ." Mrs. Secord said.

"Your husband?"

"He was wounded at the battle of Queenston Heights."

"Many fine men fell there," FitzGibbon said solemnly.

I knew a few of those men, but I was sure who FitzGibbon was thinking about—General Brock. He'd fallen leading a charge to the top of the Heights when Queenston was taken. The Lieutenant always talked about the General. He called him the bravest man he'd ever had the honour to meet. For my part, I couldn't even imagine a man more brave than FitzGibbon.

"My poor husband. Sitting in the kitchen, hearing bits and snatches of the American plans. He wanted to come himself and warn you but his leg is still not strong enough to support his weight for more than a few steps. That's why I had to come . . . no one else could do it."

"I appreciate you coming to warn me. Do I under-stand that you walked all the way here from Queenston?"

She nodded her head.

"That is over twenty miles."

"Twenty miles as the crow flies, but longer because of the route I was forced to travel. I couldn't risk coming directly."

"Then you must be terribly exhausted."

"I am very tired . . . but more than that I was feeling hopeless. I was afraid that I wouldn't find you . . . or wouldn't find you in time."

"And what precisely were the plans that you heard, Mrs. Secord?"

"They were talking about how you and your men were staying at the DeCew mill. That the DeCews were providing you with shelter and food."

Mrs. DeCew, standing off to the side, looked worried, and with good reason. If the Americans believed they'd been helping FitzGibbon, then they would surely seek retribution against her family. I'm sure she envisioned their house and mill in flames.

"They talked about the number of men who would be coming. I couldn't be certain exactly, because they didn't seem sure either—the number kept changing and growing—but I think they were talking about between four and six hundred men."

"You must have heard wrong!" I exclaimed.

Mrs. Secord shook her head. "Those were the numbers I heard."

"That actually makes sense," FitzGibbon said. "The Americans are not likely to leave the safety of Fort George unless they have sufficient numbers to bolster their courage. And they said they were going to be leaving right away?"

"That was a subject of even more debate. One of the officers wanted to delay for a few days, or even a week, while two of the others felt it best to leave immediately."

"Which means they could be here before nightfall, or not for another week," FitzGibbon said.

"Or not at all," Mrs. Secord said. "Perhaps I was overhearing nothing more than the idle bragging of a bunch of men whose tongues were lubricated by liquor."

"Perhaps," FitzGibbon agreed.

"And if that is the case, then I've been nothing but a fool . . . a silly fool."

FitzGibbon reached out and took one of Mrs. Secord's hands. "My dear woman, you walked over twenty miles, unarmed, through wild country inhabited by snakes and all manner of wild beasts, crossing enemy lines, risking your life and the home and safety of your family if the Americans were to discover your actions. You are nothing less than a hero, even if no American ever advances on our position. Every soldier under my command is beholden to you for your bravery."

Mrs. Secord looked down at her cup of tea. A small smile creased her face and she began to blush.

"Mrs. DeCew," FitzGibbon called. "Do you have a bed for Mrs. Secord?"

"Of course," she answered.

"She will require a few days' rest before she has regained sufficient strength to return to her home."

"Thank you for your concern, Lieutenant, but I will need to leave much sooner than that. My family needs me."

"As you wish. You must rest for the day and night. In the morning I'll arrange for an escort to take you at least part way home. Now if you'll excuse me, ma'am, I must take my leave and make plans in the event that we have *other guests.* Uninvited guests. And my thanks. If they do arrive, at least their arrival will not come as a surprise."

* * *

THE REST of the day saw a swarm of activity. Mounted patrols were sent out in all directions and returned with news—no Americans had been seen moving on our position. A council was held with FitzGibbon and Captain Ducharme. Messengers were sent out to notify William Merritt and his militia about the possible danger and to see how quickly they could come to the DeCews' farm if needed.

I watched as Captain Ducharme rode off. I was curious to know what he and FitzGibbon had talked about. As casually as I could, I strolled up to the Lieutenant's tent. He was seated at a table, looking at a map spread out in front of him. I coughed to get his attention.

He looked up at me. "I was wondering what was taking you so long to come and poke your nose in here."

I felt my cheeks flush. He smiled and then motioned for me to come into the tent. I took an empty seat at the table.

"I've stationed pickets on this side of the camp. Captain Ducharme has placed his men in position here, here and here," he said pointing to three other spots on the map. "And of course he has also sent patrols much farther afield. Hardly a deer could move through the woods without his native patrols being aware of it, so there is no fear of a large and noisy contingent of American soldiers going unnoticed."

That was reassuring. "Do you think anything is going to come of all this?"

"I try not to predict. My grandmother used to say, 'Pray for the best and prepare for the worst.'"

FitzGibbon stopped at the sound of horses being driven hard, hooves pounding against the ground. We both stood and hurried out of the tent in time to see three horses being reined to a stop directly in front of us. Their riders leaped down and rushed over to where we stood.

"Do you have news?" FitzGibbon demanded.

"The Americans have been spotted, sir."

"Who saw them?"

"A patrol of Caughnawagas."

"And did the Americans see our patrol?"

"They didn't think so, sir."

"How many Americans did they believe were in the party?"

"At least four hundred, possibly five hundred men. And cannons."

"I was not expecting cannons. Most peculiar tactical move. How many?"

"Three."

"Where are they?"

"They're about ten miles south of us at—"

"South!" FitzGibbon interrupted. "Are you sure of that?"

"Yes sir."

"Then we don't have much time. Not that much is needed. We're badly outnumbered and they're supported with cannon. We have only one choice."

There certainly seemed like only one choice to me. I should get back to the tent and pack my—

"We have to attack."

CHAPTER EIGHTEEN

ID HE say "attack"? Had I heard him wrong?

"I need one of you to ride after Captain Ducharme. He left no more than a few minutes before your arrival. The other two are to find William Merritt. His camp is at the fork of Twelve Mile Creek. You're to tell both men that we are going to engage the enemy at . . . come," he directed as he rushed back into his tent for the map. We all followed and in our haste to enter bumped into each other.

"Right here is the point of engagement. Beaver Dams. From the south, this is the route they must follow to get to the DeCews'. There is a large clearing just past the dam with excellent cover on all sides. We can fire from behind trees, while the Americans will have no protection from our shot. And if we need to, we can simple dissolve into the forest. At both ends of the clearing the path is narrow, twisting and obstructed. Far too narrow to allow five hundred men to move quickly. At this point," he said, placing his finger on the map, "I need Captain Ducharme to position his forces to block the enemy's retreat."

"You don't want them to retreat?" I asked, amazed.

"Perhaps . . . but only when we are ready for a retreat. We don't want them to run until we have at least given them a bloody nose." He moved his hand to another point on the map. "And if William Merritt can arrive in time, he is to come along this path, placing himself between the clearing and the DeCew farm. Is this all clear?"

Everybody nodded in agreement.

"You are dismissed. God's speed."

They rushed from the tent and within seconds I heard them leaving, riding hard. FitzGibbon had his head down, studying the map. He looked up at me.

"You believe it would be better to retreat?"

I nodded my head.

"I considered that option. I could easily withdraw my forces into the forest. We could retreat in complete safety. The Americans would have no way of following us."

That was what I wanted to do . . . disappear into the forest.

"Unfortunately that would allow the Americans to come unobstructed to the DeCew farm."

"But we'd all be gone by then," I reasoned.

"Yes, we'd be gone, but what about the DeCews?"

"They can come with us when we leave."

"But what we'll leave behind is evidence of our encampment—hoof prints, beaten-down fields, including the spots where the tents have been pitched. And that's not all. What about the farm and the mill? You know what the Americans will do when they find evidence that the DeCews have provided us with aid."

Of course I knew what would happen.

"We would have escaped into the forest, but we wouldn't have travelled far enough to escape the sight of the smoke rising into the air. The house, the barn, the mill—even the unharvested crops would be put to the torch."

I shuddered at the thought of the DeCews losing everything. They had been so kind to me, to everybody.

"But it's more than just that. If we allow the Americans to advance this far forward without being challenged then they will become braver. They will start making advances into the countryside, away from the fort and the river. No one will be safe. That can't be allowed."

He was right. "Can William Merritt and his militia get here on time?"

"I plan to engage the enemy long enough for him to arrive to reinforce our positions."

"And we can slow them down, right?" I asked.

"We can slow them down. With the fifty men of the Bully Boys and Ducharme's natives we'll be able to surround them with over one hundred and fifty men."

"Why only one hundred and fifty? Where are the rest of Captain Ducharme's men?" He'd had over two hundred warriors when we'd travelled with them!

"The Indian regiments aren't as structured as regular militia units. Warriors come and go at different times. Captain Ducharme has had as many as three hundred warriors and as few as fifty. We'd better get going." He paused and looked at me. "*I* have to get going. You don't have to come along, Tommy. I'm not sure you'll be any safer here than you'd be with me. But I'd understand if you didn't want to be close to a battle right now."

He was right again. I didn't want to be near the fighting, but I was afraid to admit it, even to myself. I wasn't a coward, I knew I wasn't, but I didn't know if I could face another battle. And this was the strangest part: I wasn't afraid that somebody would shoot at me, I was afraid that I might have to shoot at somebody else. And of course I'd heard stories, not just from FitzGibbon but from men around the campfire at night, describing the aftermath of battle. What would it be like to walk through a field littered with corpses, to hear the cries of the wounded, to know that people I knew—people like Mr. McCann or McAdams or Jamison—could or would be among them?

"You can remain here. There are things to be packed in preparation for a move in the event we can't hold them."

He had given me the opportunity to stay.

"Or you can accompany me. I'll be taking up a position away from the clearing, on a small hill. It is high enough for me to see the field of battle and the surrounding countryside. That will enable me to make decisions concerning our strategy—if we should allow the enemy to retreat, or disengage and retreat ourselves. We'll be out of range of the muskets and I can't imagine they'll even notice us, so we won't warrant cannon fire."

A shiver ran up my spine. I'd forgotten all about the cannon. I'd heard of the devastation they could do. A single cannon ball could plough through a dozen men, ripping them to shreds.

"Well, Tommy?" FitzGibbon asked.

I took a deep breath. "I want to stay here."

"I understand."

"But I'm coming with you," I said.

FitzGibbon reached out and put a hand on my shoulder.

* * *

WE LEFT our horses tied to a branch at the bottom of the hill. As we climbed, I watched the rest of the Bully Boys move along the path toward the clearing. They were going to take their mounts slightly farther along and then take cover in the forest at the end of the clearing and along the path leading away from it. I felt better knowing that those fifty men stood between me and the Americans. There was nobody, on either side of the border, more brave and loyal and strong than FitzGibbon's men. I had nothing to fear . . . and then I remembered that there were over five hundred Americans. Even the Bully Boys couldn't fight against odds that high.

"Here, take these," FitzGibbon said.

He handed me a pair of field glasses, just like his. I put them up to my eyes and could no longer find the clearing, which I'd seen so well in the distance. I moved them closer and then farther from my eyes until they came into focus. Then I looked around until I finally spotted the opening in the forest.

"Do you see anything?" FitzGibbon asked.

"Nothing."

"Neither do I," he admitted.

"Do you think they're coming?" Perhaps there was still a chance that they had turned around. Or maybe they were coming some other way . . . coming at us from another direction. That thought sent a chill through my body.

"They'll be coming."

"Maybe they've turned around."

FitzGibbon chuckled softly. "Not likely. I'm still surprised, though, that they chose this route to the DeCews'. It's much longer, not very well known and . . . I wonder."

"What?"

"It's the sort of trail known only by locals. I wonder if they are being led by a traitor, perhaps even the infamous Dr. Cyrenius Chapin himself."

I lowered the field glasses and looked over at FitzGibbon. "Do you really think it could be him?"

FitzGibbon's eyes remained riveted to his field glasses, staring at the clearing. "Him or some other traitor. Men like that turn my stomach. What I have to remember is that for every one like him there are dozens and dozens of others. People of integrity and honour and loyalty, like William Merritt and Mrs. Secord, and your father . . . and you."

I suddenly felt very uncomfortable. "Will we have to wait long?" I stammered, wanting desperately to change the subject.

"Not long. Look for yourself. The first of the American column has entered the clearing."

CHAPTER NINETEEN

I PUT THE field glasses back up to my eyes and wildly scanned the distance, trying to see the oncoming Americans. I found the entrance into the clearing. It was marked by a blue stain which was spreading as I watched. Twenty or thirty mounted soldiers had already entered the clearing, two abreast. I had somehow just assumed it would be infantry. How many cavalrymen did they have, and could we get away from them if they came after us? Almost in answer to my unspoken prayer the line of cavalry ended and foot soldiers proceeded into the clearing, four or five of them spread out across the path. I started to count but I stopped after the fifteenth row.

What was the point? It was obvious that we were badly outnumbered. I let my eyes wander to the far end of the clearing. There was still a long open space before the cavalry got to the far side, but was there enough space for the entire column of soldiers to enter?

"There's the first of the cannons," FitzGibbon said.

I scanned back to the opening. A pair of horses was pulling a gun carriage. Directly behind it was a second pair of horses with another cannon. Then the ranks of foot soldiers started again.

"When will we open fire?" I asked.

"If they follow orders they'll wait until the first men in line, the cavalry, get almost to this side of the clearing."

"But what if the rest of the column hasn't entered in the clearing by then?"

"No matter. Those still on the path will come running to the clearing like the devil is on their tail once the Caughnawagas start whooping and hollering and shooting at them."

"But won't the cavalry try to break out toward the DeCews'?"

FitzGibbon shook his head. "Not likely. And even if they do they won't get far. We've strung ropes across the path at waist height and strewn rocks and logs all along one section so that no horse will make it through. The soldiers would have to dismount and come under our—"

The retort of a musket called out and then echoed across the clearing, sounding like distant thunder. There was a split second of silence and then an explosion of fire. Shot after shot rang out. The clearing was a rush of motion. The cavalry swung around, back toward the main body of the column. On the ground lay a horse, while half a dozen other horses ran without riders.

Some of the shot had found its mark. The American foot soldiers broke ranks and swarmed around the gun carriages. A cloud of smoke rose over the clearing and men were dropping to their knees or to the ground. A couple fell as though they'd been shot. The last of a stream of blue uniforms entered the clearing and joined the mass of men who had formed into a circle in the middle, with three gun carriages and two supply wagons at the centre. The cloud of smoke thickened above the clearing, partially obstructing my view of the Americans, as the shooting continued. I saw some flashes from the forest, where our men had fired, but as I scanned the forest I couldn't see anybody. They were lost among the trees and bushes.

All at once a group of American soldiers broke free of

the mass and started moving toward the edge of the clearing, trying to make for the cover of the trees. A barrage of fire was directed toward them and I saw the whole front of the line fall to the ground. It surged forward a few more feet, and some of those who had taken the lead fell as well. The column broke and dissolved, and those men still standing ran back to rejoin the main group, leaving the bodies of their fallen comrades strewn upon the ground.

I could clearly see the entire battle playing out before me, hear the retorts of the guns, even smell the shot, but somehow none of it seemed real. It was more like a dream, or something I was reading about in an old history book.

"This is the time for action," FitzGibbon said.

"What do you mean?" I asked anxiously.

"I have to get down to the battlefield."

"Are you going to allow them to retreat now?"

"Hardly."

FitzGibbon ran toward our horses. I stood in place. Was I to wait there? Should I follow? I didn't want to go, but I didn't want to stay alone.

I ran after him and got to my horse just in time to see him galloping off down the path. I leaped up onto my grey and gave chase. He was lost from my sight as he rounded the first curve in the twisting, turning path. Then I suddenly remembered what FitzGibbon had said about debris being thrown on the path and ropes strung across it. I reined in my horse, slowing to a canter. Maybe FitzGibbon could go faster because he had some idea where the traps were set, but I couldn't. Besides, why did I need to rush toward the battle? I wasn't even carrying a weapon. I hadn't even held a gun since . . . since that day.

Maybe, I thought, I shouldn't even go. I knew I could just stop, turn my horse around and leave. That thought was warm and reassuring. I could ride away from the battle. I wasn't a soldier. I was just a kid. Nobody would blame me if I went back to the camp. Nobody would think anything of it. Nobody would think that I was . . . was a coward. But at that moment I felt like one. I laughed. FitzGibbon had said I was a hero. He'd compared me to William Merritt and Mrs. Secord and my Pa. I was no hero. I was scared.

And then I remembered something FitzGibbon had said to me. It had been only a few weeks ago, but it seemed as though years had passed: "The difference between a brave man and a coward is not how he feels, but what he does despite those feelings."

I dug in my heels and spurred my mount forward to

the battle. I galloped around the curve, my horse's hooves throwing up dirt as we ate up the distance. Just beyond the next turn there was a line of horses—the mounts of the regiment. The reins were all attached to one long line held by a single knot. The release of that knot would set all the horses free.

FitzGibbon's horse was there, but he was nowhere to be seen. I jumped off my horse, wrapped the reins once around a branch and ran down the path toward the field of battle. It was at least a good twenty or thirty paces away through thick forest, and I still couldn't see it, but I could hear the sounds of the musket fire and the bitter smell of sulphur hung in the air. I ducked under a rope strung across the path, dodged around some bushes and logs and rounded another corner.

FitzGibbon was standing in the middle of the path. Around him were five members of his company. I slowed to a walk. He was holding a pole, and on the top of the pole was a large, white flag. What was he up to?

I moved close enough to hear them talking.

"I want every man to be in position, loaded, and have a man targeted as I head out," FitzGibbon said.

"Don't move out until they stop shooting," McWilliams said.

"And when they start coming you make sure you don't walk too fast or too far," Jamison added.

"I'll be walking as slowly as I can," FitzGibbon said.

It was now obvious to me what was happening—he was going to walk into the clearing under a flag of truce. What I still didn't know was what he planned to talk about, but knowing FitzGibbon it might have been almost anything.

"Get to your positions. Make sure everybody holds their fire. All I *don't* need when I'm out there is for somebody to open fire so that I get caught in the middle of a hail of shot."

The men all rushed off to their positions and I walked to FitzGibbon's side. I wanted an answer to my question.

"Hold this for a second, would you?" FitzGibbon said as he handed me the pole. I took it from him and watched as he removed his jacket and pulled on one that had been on the ground by his feet. It had a Captain's insignia on the sleeve!

"What are you doing?" I asked.

"This is what they call a field promotion."

"You've become a captain?" I asked in amazement.

"Not yet, but I thought a captain would make a better impression. A captain is in charge of more men, and I want them to think they're up against a sizeable force. That will buy us more time. Perhaps enough to allow William Merritt's militia and more natives to arrive. We might also find out just how determined our adversary is."

"You mean, sort of like you did with the militia unit across the river?"

"Exactly. My old granny always said, you have two ears and one mouth because you're to listen twice as much as you talk. I want to hear what they have to say. I'd better get going. Give me the flag," he said, reaching out to take it from me.

I held on. "Shouldn't a high-ranking officer like a captain have somebody else holding the flag of truce?"

"You?"

I nodded. "I'm already holding it."

"I could always get somebody else," he suggested.

"Everybody else is holding a gun. Wouldn't it be best not to sacrifice any marksmen?"

FitzGibbon nodded his head slowly. "Are you sure you want to come with me? You don't have to."

"I know. Let's go . . . before I change my mind."

We walked down the path, stepping around the rocks and logs. From this distance the sound of the gunshots was much louder, but I noticed that it was no longer a solid barrage. I could now make out individual shots. I caught sight of movement off to the side. Looking over, I saw two Bully Boys moving through the bush toward the edge of the clearing. We came to a stop just before the cover ended. The path entered into the clearing on an angle so I couldn't see the Americans . . . and they couldn't see me.

"Wait for the bugler to sound cease fire," FitzGibbon said.

"We have a bugler?"

FitzGibbon chuckled. "Same as the captain's jacket. Just another trick to convince the enemy we are more than meets the eye."

Almost immediately the sound of the bugle blared out, echoing through the trees. The blasts of gunfire lessened, dropped to a few shots and then stopped altogether.

"When we step out, you have to hold the flag over your head as high as you can and wave it in the air."

"I can do that."

"And if they direct any shot at us, you drop the flag and crawl, flat on your belly, and don't stop crawling until you've passed a dozen feet into the trees. Understand?"

"I understand."

"Then let's go."

FitzGibbon started to walk out into the open and I reached out and grabbed him by the arm. "The flag has to lead," I said.

"You do like to be in the middle of things," FitzGibbon observed.

"Only when I have to be."

I walked to the very edge of the clearing. With the flag held high and out in front of me I stepped into the meadow. I held the pole at the very end, hoisting it even higher and waving it more wildly. This seemed almost crazy—trying to draw the attention of hundreds of armed Americans!

Men were holding their fire. Silence. FitzGibbon stepped out beside me.

"Do we start walking toward them?" I asked.

"No. We just stay here and wait until we see their flag of truce. Then we move forward at the same time they come to us. We want to meet close to the middle."

I nodded. Stretched out in front of us was the entire mass of Americans. One of the cannons was aimed almost right where we stood.

"That big gun could get us here easily, couldn't it?" I said.

"Cut us in two practically. But we're also within musket range. Probably five or six soldiers have each of us in their sights, waiting."

"Waiting for what?" I asked in alarm.

"Waiting for somebody to start shooting. If we shoot their messengers, then they shoot us. And here they come."

Two men were coming forward. One was waving a white handkerchief tied to a sword held high above his head. We started walking toward them. I felt a wave of uncertainty as we left the cover of the forest behind. Now if the firing started I couldn't simply throw myself to the ground and crawl a few feet into the trees. We stopped, as did the Americans, with a dozen feet between us.

"You requested a truce," one of the Americans said. "What do you wish to say?"

"There are things to discuss," FitzGibbon said, "but I am not prepared to discuss anything with a junior officer!"

"I am a lieutenant, and—"

"And I am a captain!" FitzGibbon snapped. "Are you able to make decisions and speak with authority for your side?"

"No, the Colonel is the one who would make those—"

"I will not discuss things with a subordinate officer

with no authority! You are dismissed, Lieutenant! You may return to your ranks and we will also retreat. No discussion will take place!"

FitzGibbon turned and started to walk away.

"Wait!" the American officer called out.

FitzGibbon stopped and turned around.

"I will get my superior."

"Good. We will retreat and await your response."

The Americans started back to their ranks and we started to walk toward the trees.

"Slow down," FitzGibbon said.

I lessened my pace. I knew I'd been hurrying. I didn't want to leave my back exposed to the Americans for any longer than necessary.

"Why wouldn't you talk to him?" I asked.

"It's no use talking to people who can't make decisions. Besides, by doing this I've bought us some more time. Time is on our side."

Finally we reached the cover of the trees and I breathed a sigh of relief. I lowered the flag of truce to the ground. I flexed my fingers. Two members of the Bully Boys rushed up to us.

"Good news, sir," one of them announced. "Reinforcements have arrived."

"William Merritt?"

"No, sir. Captain Hall arrived from Chippawa with twenty men, and William Kerr, and—"

"William Kerr is here!" FitzGibbon exclaimed.

"Yes, sir, with almost one hundred warriors from the Six Nations."

"But how did they even know about the Americans?"

"He said he and his men were tracking the American forces, and then they just came upon the battle after we'd engaged the enemy."

FitzGibbon started to laugh.

"Sir, the Americans are waving their flag of truce again," one of the soldiers announced.

"Good! I'm now even more eager to engage them in discussion. Come, Tommy!"

I picked up the pole and hurried after FitzGibbon, who was striding across the meadow quickly. There were two men, riding horses, one with an officer's black felt hat, coming toward us.

"Shouldn't we slow down?" I suggested.

"No. We want to look confident and in charge."

We stopped just before the Americans.

"Good day, sir, my name is Boerstler, Colonel Boerstler."

My goodness, I thought. They had skipped up from lieutenant, past captain and major all the way to colonel! Now we were outranked.

"It was not necessary to send the commanding officer," FitzGibbon said.

"Perhaps not," Colonel Boerstler said. "And your name and rank?"

"I am a captain. Captain James FitzGibbon."

"FitzGibbon?" Colonel Boerstler questioned. "Of the Green Tigers?"

"Yes, sir. I was told that this expedition was directed toward me and my men. That is why my commanding officer directed me to meet with you under a flag of truce. I have been given full authority to negotiate terms and conditions."

The Colonel's mount shifted to the side and I saw blood staining a bandage binding his thigh. He'd been hit. FitzGibbon must have seen it too.

"You called for this truce, Captain FitzGibbon. I assume you are going to suggest we disengage. I will put forward the position that I am willing to withdraw my forces."

"I'm sorry, Colonel, but that is not an option. I am here to request your surrender."

"Surrender!"

My mouth almost dropped open and I had to stifle a gasp. This was unbelievable . . . for anybody except Fitz-Gibbon. I'd seen him bluff his way through things before, but nothing this big.

"And what makes you believe that we would be prepared to accept such terms?" the Colonel demanded.

I wanted to hear this myself.

"I am simply appealing to your good judgment and your understanding of the situation in which you find yourself," FitzGibbon said. His voice was calm and quiet.

"And just how do you perceive our situation?" Colonel Boerstler asked.

"You are surrounded, have inferior position lacking in cover, have no hope of reinforcements and are confronted by a greater number of men," FitzGibbon explained.

"I do not believe you have more men than my force, Captain. I would estimate your numbers to be no more than one half of those under my command."

"That is very astute of you, Colonel. At the beginning of the battle we had only about three hundred men. Subsequently our reinforcements have arrived. You are now surrounded by nearly eight hundred men."

"You are bluffing, Captain FitzGibbon! There are not

eight hundred British soldiers between here and Burlington Bay!"

"I said nothing about British soldiers. The mass of men under my command are Indians."

"Indians? I haven't seen more than three dozen natives."

"I'm surprised you have seen even that many. That is one of the gifts of my native brothers. They have the ability to blend into the forest, unseen . . . unseen, that is, until they end your life." There was a pause, filled by the impact of the words that FitzGibbon had just spoken.

"The natives are good soldiers. Easy to command, but difficult to hold to the conventions of war."

"What do you mean?" Colonel Boerstler questioned.

"Once the battle begins in earnest they are difficult to rein in. I was most fortunate that they refrained from firing during this truce. Their hatred for Americans is genuine and, I must admit, understandable. I'm afraid that they do not believe in prisoners . . . or survivors. When we re-engage they will not stop fighting until not one enemy is left standing."

Colonel Boerstler's expression showed no emotion. Did he believe FitzGibbon's bluff? Or was it a bluff? He sounded so convincing that I wasn't completely sure myself.

"I will not surrender to a force that I have not observed. Have your forces step into the clearing so that I may see your numbers."

FitzGibbon laughed. "Unacceptable. We will not reveal our positions."

The Colonel turned away from FitzGibbon and looked directly at me. "Is he bluffing?"

"Excuse me?" I stammered.

"Is he bluffing? Does he really have that many men?"

"You're asking me?"

"Yes, I've heard tales of FitzGibbon's cunning. You're just a lad. You I can believe."

I turned to FitzGibbon. He nodded, giving me permission to talk.

"I don't know. I'm not even a regular soldier."

"But you do have regular eyes. Tell me what you've seen."

I took a deep breath and thought through my answer. "I don't know how many men there are, sir, but I know there are the Bully Boys, and William Merritt's militia, and reinforcements from Chippawa, and Captain Ducharme's Caughnawagas, and William Kerr, and the warriors from the Six Nations. And there are probably more who have arrived since we came out under the truce." I paused. "Could I ask you a question, sir?"

He looked a little startled by my request. "Certainly, son."

I reached into my pocket and pulled out the letter. "I was given this letter by a dying American soldier. He asked if I could give it to his wife and tell her and their children what happened and that he loved them."

Colonel Boerstler reached out his hand. "That is very considerate of you, son. I'll make sure she receives it."

I drew back the letter. "Oh, no, sir, you don't understand. It isn't that I think you'll be able to pass on a letter, sir. I wanted to know if there was anything *you* wanted me to pass on to your wife or loved ones."

The Colonel's mouth dropped open in shock.

"Colonel, we have no further time for discussion," FitzGibbon stated, jumping into the gap. "Do you surrender, sir?"

"I . . . I require time to think. You shall have your answer . . . by sundown."

"Unacceptable and unadvisable," FitzGibbon interrupted. "I cannot possibly guarantee control of the native warriors that long. You must make your decision, *now*."

"I cannot do that!" Colonel Boerstler objected.

"Fine. We have made our offer. The death of your men is no longer on my head. The consequences are now yours and yours alone! Good day, sir!" FitzGibbon spun around and started to walk away. I stumbled after him.

"Wait!" Colonel Boerstler called out.

FitzGibbon stopped and turned back. The two men looked at each other without speaking.

"I am prepared to surrender my forces. I ask for a period of twenty minutes to advise my men and prepare to lay down our arms. Is that acceptable?"

FitzGibbon nodded his head slowly. "I accept both your terms . . . and your surrender."

CHAPTER TWENTY

I SAT ON the grass. The sun shone down brightly. It felt good. I felt good. And relaxed, for the first time in over two weeks. It had taken that long for all the American prisoners to be transported to other locations. Five hundred and forty-two prisoners. That number still boggled my mind. While close to one hundred of them were wounded and required medical aid, the remainder were healthy—healthy enough to be dangerous—and were being guarded by a much smaller number of men. I hadn't slept well thinking about what would happen if they tried to escape. Even without weapons they would still have overrun us, I was sure.

I had gone with the Lieutenant, who was still a captain in their eyes, and walked among the prisoners. Their colonel was in the medical tent receiving treatment for the wound to his thigh. I was happy when I learned that he wasn't going to lose his leg. I enjoyed our conversations, and I did feel badly about tricking him . . . but then again, it might have saved his life, and mine. The Lieutenant told me that he thought what I said to the Colonel made the difference in him accepting the terms of surrender. I didn't like to say that myself . . . but maybe he was right.

There was one prisoner who I was glad to see under heavy guard—Captain Chapin! FitzGibbon had danced a jig when he first discovered Dr. Cyrenius Chapin among the American prisoners. The Lieutenant held a deep hatred for the man. Loyalty came to FitzGibbon as naturally as breath, and he couldn't stomach a traitor. Chapin was kept separate from the other prisoners. A special fate, a hangman's rope, awaited him, and all traitors to the Crown, in Kingston.

When I first saw Captain Chapin I was surprised. I don't know what I was expecting—maybe horns and hoofed feet! The day before he was shipped out I heard him talking to his guards. He sounded like anybody else, except for maybe being a little bit nervous. He looked over at me when I was looking at him and he smiled. I thought I'd feel hatred toward him, or at least anger, for all the things he'd done. But I didn't. Instead I just felt sorry for him, and for his family. Nobody in this war was much different from anybody else. That was something that seemed to become clearer in my mind all the time.

My thoughts were interrupted by the sound of thunder. I looked up and scanned the horizon, but there wasn't a cloud in the sky. How could there be thunder? Another blast. There must have been a storm brewing somewhere. It was best that I got back to work before it arrived. The fields weren't going to harvest themselves.

*　　*　　*

I'D FILLED no more than half a dozen baskets of corn when I was stopped by the sound of approaching horses. My first thought was that it might be American soldiers, but I realized that wasn't a great possibility. I was told that since the defeat in the clearing at Beaver Dams the Americans had hardly ventured out of sight of Fort George.

I recognized Mr. McCann, along with two other

riders. They were coming fast. Mr. McCann reined in his horse, bringing it to a stop directly in front of me, while the other two riders rode off without him.

"Are you interested in going for a ride?" he asked. There was an urgency to his voice that alarmed me. Were there more Americans coming?

"Where to?"

"To investigate."

I gave him a questioning look.

"Where there's smoke there's usually fire," Mr. McCann said. He motioned over his shoulder.

There in the distance was a thick column of smoke rising up into the sky. I'd been so intent upon the harvest, my eyes to the ground, that I hadn't noticed.

"What is it? What's burning?"

"That we don't know. It's in the general direction of Queenston. What doesn't make sense, though, are the explosions that we heard just before the smoke."

"Explosions! I thought that was thunder!"

He shook his head. "Gunpowder. The Americans are up to some mischief. It looks to be taking place close to Fort George and Queenston."

My thoughts raced back to my farm. Had it been set on fire, or Mr. McCann's store?

"There's no point in thinking the worst," Mr. McCann said, reading my mind. "We'll know soon enough. Advance scouts have already gone out. The Lieutenant is assembling a second group of riders now."

We both heard the sound of approaching horses and watched as they broke through the trees. FitzGibbon was at the head of a column of two dozen men. They had traded their more common grey coats and were dressed in brilliant red, so that they looked like a flame bursting through the forest. I could only imagine the fear an American would feel seeing them charging toward him.

The Lieutenant waved to us, a smile on his face. We waved back. I could almost feel the excitement I knew he was feeling.

There was a gap and then another column of men, all militia, followed. I tried to count but stopped when the number reached thirty. I knew I'd feel safe with such a large group going before us. At the very end was Jamison, and he was leading my grey behind him!

"The Lieutenant said he couldn't imagine you'd say no to the invitation so he had your horse saddled," Mr. McCann said with a smile.

Jamison came to a stop right in front of us as the remaining columns raced away. I took the reins. I couldn't help but notice that a rifle had been attached to the saddle. Any thought that somehow this might just be a pleasure ride was erased from my mind. I climbed aboard and we spurred our horses onward. I didn't know about Mr. McCann or Jamison, but I wanted to be in the company of the large group of soldiers. They were moving fast and we pushed our horses harder to catch them. As the path twisted and turned they'd move out of sight, coming back into view only as we hit longer, straight sections. I was surprised not only at their pace but at their choice of routes. Rather than taking a little-used trail they were moving toward the main road to Queenston. FitzGibbon *never* took the major roads!

We moved hard until we came to the road. Up ahead I could see that the first riders had dismounted and they were watering their horses from a small stream that ran beside the roadway. We caught the group and also dismounted to allow our horses to rest and water. It was not just kind, but clever to give them rest. If we rode hard and then were confronted by Americans we'd need the animals to be fresh enough to carry us to safety.

"Could you watch my horse?" I asked Mr. McCann. "I want to talk to the Lieutenant."

"I can if you'll share his answers with me!"

Despite everything I couldn't help but laugh.

FitzGibbon stood on the road, staring into the distance. The column of smoke was now thicker, dominating the sky.

"I didn't think you'd decline my invitation."

"I'm curious too . . . but why are we taking the road?" I asked him.

"A straight line is the fastest."

"But what about American patrols?"

"Last week they pulled back their pickets to a spot much closer to the fort. This is now a safe route for us to—" He stopped. "Riders approaching!"

I looked down the road. I couldn't see anybody, but I could see a plume of dust rising into the air.

FitzGibbon barked out orders and everybody leaped into action. The horses were quickly led off to cover by half a dozen men while the rest took up positions behind the trees on both sides of the road. I removed the rifle from my horse before she was taken. I took my place next to FitzGibbon, behind a fallen log.

"Do you think it's Americans?" I asked.

"I don't know, but we have to be prepared."

"What if it's a lot of Americans?" There were close to fifty of us, but there could have been four hundred of them.

"If it is a sizeable force, we'll cut it down in a hurry," FitzGibbon said as he steadied his rifle along the top of the log, taking aim at the road. "Either way, we won't have long to wait."

I strained my eyes to see up the road. I was relieved when I realized it didn't look like a big party. No more than three or four riders . . . wearing red coats! They were our men.

The soldiers farther up the road had also seen that they were British and had started to come out from their hiding spots. There were three horsemen and they came to a stop in our midst. It was obvious that the horses had been ridden hard as they were frothing at the mouth.

"What is in front of us?" FitzGibbon demanded.

"An open road with no Americans," one of the men answered.

"None?"

"Neither on the road nor in the countryside."

"For how far?"

"We were sent back with Queenston in sight. The Sergeant had the men take up positions along the road, awaiting your arrival."

"It sounds as if the Americans might have pulled

back even farther. Did you discover the source of the smoke?" FitzGibbon asked. "Is it coming from the village?"

"We didn't get close enough to see what was burning."

FitzGibbon nodded his head. "Everybody mount up."

There was a scramble as the men found their horses and reassembled on the road. FitzGibbon ordered the men to ride four abreast, with spacing between each group. He took the lead, followed by the rest of the red-coated Bully Boys and then the militia members. Mr. McCann was as anxious as anybody to find out what awaited us, but he was probably still under orders to stay by my side, and we fell in at the very end of the column.

I knew this road well. We brought crops to market in the fall along this route. More often, though, we travelled it by horse-drawn sleigh. Almost all our visiting to friends and family was done in winter. The rest of the year there was always too much to be done around the farm to travel even a dozen miles afield.

We were moving at a good clip and quickly closing the distance to Queenston. I recognized where we were, and knew we were no more than a mile from the houses on the outskirts of the village. The smoke in the sky was becoming more pronounced, and the smell of it intertwined with the smell of the dust being thrown up by the horses in front of us.

Up ahead I saw the big barn of the McKenzie farm. There was a healthy-looking crop being harvested. Everything looked fine.

"Whooooaaaa!" came the call from the front of the column, and we came to a halt. What was happening? Had the enemy been spotted?

Before I had time to even think anything further we started to move again. But looking up ahead I saw that FitzGibbon was dispersing the men. He was splitting the group up, sending one party of men off to the left and a second off to the right. He held up his hand as we approached.

"Well?" Mr. McCann asked.

"Nothing. No American pickets yet. The question remains whether they have men still posted in the village or if they have pulled back, right inside the walls of the fort."

"How will we know?" I asked.

"There's only one way." He paused. "We have to enter the village. I've sent the men to take up positions surrounding Queenston. I'm going in."

"By yourself?"

"Possibly with one other man . . . somebody who knows the village," he said, looking at Mr. McCann.

"It would be my pleasure," he answered.

"How about with two other men?" I suggested.

"I suspected you would suggest as much," FitzGibbon said.

Slowly we moved forward, FitzGibbon of course slightly in front. He pulled his rifle from the holster and laid it across his lap. Mr. McCann did the same, and reluctantly I followed suit. We moved past the first few houses. There was fresh wash hanging on a line behind one of the houses, flapping in the breeze. There was no other sound except the soft clumping of the hooves of our horses.

"That's a beautiful sight," Mr. McCann said.

"What is?" FitzGibbon asked. I already knew the answer.

"My store."

"Ah, yes, I know your store well," FitzGibbon said. He looked back at me with a smile, and despite the situation I couldn't help smiling back, thinking about where my adventure had begun.

"There's been more than one time when I didn't think I would live to see it again, or that it would be there for me to see," Mr. McCann said softly.

"It looks fine," I said. "Everything looks fine . . . untouched. But where is that smoke coming from?"

"I don't know. It almost looks like it's coming from the fort," Mr. McCann said.

"The fort? I wonder . . ." FitzGibbon said.

"Wonder what?"

"There's only one reason the fort would be on fire."

"Why? Why would the fort be on fire?" I demanded.

"I need to have a closer look," FitzGibbon said.

"Closer? Is that safe?"

"If my guess is right it's perfectly safe. I want you to wait here." Without warning, FitzGibbon dug in his heels and his horse leaped forward.

"Where! Where are you going?" I yelled.

"To the fort!" he screamed over his shoulder.

"The fort!" Mr. McCann said. "He can't go to the fort alone!"

"He isn't!" I said.

I was about to spur my horse forward when Mr. McCann reached out and grabbed the reins. "He said to wait here."

"He was talking to you," I said.

"What makes you think that?"

"You're a soldier, he can give you orders, but not me."

"But I was also ordered to stay with you," Mr. McCann said.

"Then you should stay with me. Come on, he's almost out of sight."

FitzGibbon was now at the far end of the village. Mr. McCann flashed me a smile and dropped the reins of my horse. I dug my heels into the sides of the grey and she leaped forward. We raced forward as FitzGibbon disappeared around the turn leading to Fort George. Within a dozen seconds we'd reached the same spot. As we raced past the last house we met one of our pickets— four men who had been sent around to the far side of the village. FitzGibbon had passed by just seconds before and they were now scrambling to get onto their horses. We burst past them. FitzGibbon was now even farther ahead, his big black horse eating up the distance to the fort faster than we could close the gap.

I looked back over my shoulder and was relieved to see not just the four soldiers from the picket but at least a dozen of our men thundering after us. At least we weren't alone—although what good would twenty, or even two hundred men do against more than two thousand Americans?

Just up ahead, beyond the trees, across a long, open

meadow, was the fort. We'd soon be able to see it . . . and anybody in the fort would be able to see us. FitzGibbon again disappeared from view as he rounded the last stand of trees. The column of smoke was rising from just beyond those trees, staining the entire sky. I could taste the bitter, acidic odour of gunpowder in the air.

Of all the foolhardy things I'd done since leaving home, chasing FitzGibbon like a bat out of hell right into the waiting arms of the enemy was probably the craziest! If I got out of this alive . . .

FitzGibbon had now cleared the trees and made it to the other side, within sight of the fort, and within reach of their cannon. I had to fight the urge to pull up on my horse, either slow down to allow the others to catch us or stop completely to enable them to pass. Instead I dug my heels in harder. We burst through the last of the trees and—

"Whooooaaaa!" I screamed as we brought our horses to a stop.

FitzGibbon was right there in front of us. He'd halted his horse just a hundred feet into the clearing. I was going to say something when my mouth fell open at the sight of the fort. Thick pillars of smoke rose from within it, the front gate was wide open, wooden timbers strewn about.

And the walls, the thick stone walls, were cracked and shattered in places with gaping holes visible.

"What . . . what happened?" I stammered.

But FitzGibbon just whooped for joy and threw his hat into the air. "The Americans have destroyed the fort!" he shouted.

"But why? Why would they do that?"

"Because we've won, Tommy, because we've won. They've abandoned the fort, they've withdrawn."

"Does this mean the war . . . the war is over?" I asked in a halting voice.

"Not for everybody," FitzGibbon said, "but it is for you."

"What do you mean?"

"The Americans have withdrawn well beyond Queenston. It's safe for you to go home."

CHAPTER TWENTY-ONE

"COME ON, YAH!" I screamed as the horses dug in harder. "Yah! Yah!"

The horses surged forward again until their harness became taut and they were frozen in place, defeated by the stump, unable to move even an inch farther.

"Whoa, girls!" I called out as I backed them up slightly.

I picked up the axe and started to chop away at one of the exposed roots. The blade dug into the flesh of the stump, sending chips flying up into the air, and one glanced off the side of my face. I swung again, and again, and again, until I broke through. I dropped the axe to the ground from my sweat-soaked hands. The sun was hot, and there was hardly anything more tiring and back-breaking than clearing stumps, but each one removed freed up a few more feet of field to be ploughed and planted.

"Come on, girls . . . you can do it," I said reassuringly. "Yah! Yah!" I screamed.

They jumped forward and the harness strained. I could see the stump shaking, resisting under their power, but starting to give.

"Yah!"

There was a loud *pop* and then the stump pulled free. The horses practically jumped forward, almost stumbling, with the sudden release.

"Whoa!"

I walked to the front of the team and I reached up with one hand for each animal, to scratch behind their ears. Bessy ignored my touch, but my grey leaned her head over and pushed harder against my hand. In the beginning I wasn't sure she would ever become a farm animal, but she'd showed me she could do just about anything.

"That looks like a difficult job," a voice called out.

I turned around. It was FitzGibbon in his red uniform, sitting atop his horse! "Lieutenant!" I called as I rushed over to his side.

He climbed down from his horse and we shook hands. It had been almost six months since I'd seen the Lieutenant, and almost a full year since the last American had left Canadian soil and the terms of peace had been agreed to. Everything, all the borders, had returned to the way they'd been before the war.

"Actually, it's Captain now," FitzGibbon said, turning his arm to show me his new insignia. "And this time it isn't just a trick."

"What are you doing here?" I'd heard FitzGibbon was stationed in the town of York now.

"I had government business in these parts and I wanted to stop in and give my regards to you and your family."

"Can you visit for a while? I'm sure my Ma would be upset if you didn't stay for supper."

"That has already been arranged. I was up at the house, looking for you, and your parents extended an invitation. I see you've put your horse to good use," he said gesturing to my grey. "Did you finally give her a name?"

"Yeah . . . I call her Grey."

He laughed. "Not the most imaginative name, but fitting nonetheless."

"She's really made a difference around the farm. It would be twice as much work to clear these stumps without her," I explained.

"Even with her, it looks like a very difficult job."

"It is," I agreed. "But the only way to grow more crops is to clear more land. Whenever the horses and I aren't needed elsewhere I harness them and we come out here. It's slow, but we're doing it. I've cleared almost an acre and a half this summer."

"Your father is lucky to have such an industrious son," FitzGibbon said with a smile.

"I'm not just doing it for him," I admitted. "All the land in this direction," I said, motioning to the stand of trees, "will be mine someday. My Pa says there are forty acres for me and forty for my brother. I'm just clearing a little of it now. I hope I can make a go of it."

"Have no fear, Tommy. I know you will be a success, whether as a farmer or as something else."

"Something else?" I asked.

He nodded his head. "I must admit that this is more than just a social visit. I have been given the task of recruiting young men from the area. Men who would like to take up service for His Majesty. Be part of an enlarged standing guard."

"Are things brewing again across the border?" I asked anxiously. There were always fears of the Americans returning.

"All is quiet. I think the bloody nose we gave the Americans will stay in their minds for a long time to come."

"Then why is the size of the guard being increased?"

"Good fences make for good neighbours, and a sizeable force of men in arms tends to keep people on their own side of the fence. And of course I could think of hardly a man more deserving to be part of that force, a man who showed more bravery, than you."

I looked down at the ground, feeling honoured but also a bit embarrassed. For a moment I imagined myself in the grey uniform of FitzGibbon's Bully Boys. But at the same time my thoughts flashed back to the eyes of a dying man . . . the man I'd shot. I didn't know what to say.

"Have you thought of any future beyond the farm?"

"I used to think about it all the time. Wonder what I'd do if I left the farm."

"And now?"

"And now I know what I want to do, how I'm going to spend my life."

"You do?" FitzGibbon asked.

I nodded my head. "I'm going to be working the piece of land right beside my Pa's farm. I'm a farmer. And that's what I'm always going to be." I paused. "Unless those Americans decide to come back across that river."

FitzGibbon put a hand on my shoulder. He nodded his head slowly as if to say he not only understood but that he approved. "And a fine farmer you're going to be."

"I'll do my best."

"I know you will, Tommy. There's a time for war, and a time for peace," FitzGibbon said. "But now . . . it's time for supper! Come, let's share a meal. And I might just have a story or two to share with you!"

POSTSCRIPT

ALMOST ALL the adventures documented in this novel—from the opening scenes in the general store, to entering Fort George disguised as a peddler, to the battle at Beaver Dams—are based on the real actions of Lieutenant James FitzGibbon, a great Canadian hero.

The Bully Boys

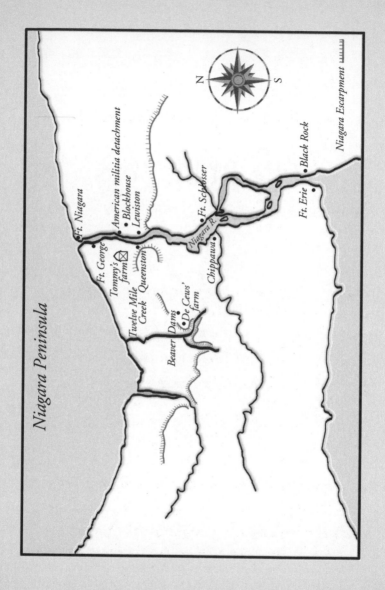

Niagara Peninsula

N S

Niagara Escarpment

Black Rock

Ft. Erie

Ft. Niagara

American militia detachment
Blockhouse
Lewiston

Ft. Schlosser

Niagara R.

Ft. George
Tommy's farm
Queenston
Twelve Mile Creek

De Cew's farm

Chippawa

Beaver Dams

An Interview with Eric Walters

What inspired you to write a story about the War of 1812?

The War of 1812 is part of the grade seven curriculum. I was teaching this unit and while I was reading a novel about the war to my students, they were falling asleep! I couldn't believe something exciting hadn't been written, so I wrote *The Bully Boys*.

What sort of influence does your former career as a teacher have on your writing?

My first 35 novels were written for my class. I'd come up with ideas related to the things I was teaching and as I wrote the books I'd share them with my students chapter by chapter. This was not only to get them more interested in reading and writing but helped me to craft books that they liked by listening to their feedback.

Why is it important for children to read stories like **The Bully Boys?**

Canada is the greatest country on Earth. Young people need to know about our heritage and the incredible people of our history so that they realize they can aspire to greatness.

When you decide to write a story set during a war, how do you handle the violent aspects of the story?

Wars are violent. To not include these scenes is to romanticize the reality and make it seem like a game. In fact, my protagonist thinks of it as a game—until he is confronted with the brutal reality of battle and death. I included one scene that the original editor wanted "softened." I wanted it left as it was because it was a very realistic view of death.

Although the novel is fiction, you include a great deal of true historical events and people. How do you create the fine balance of fact and fiction?

You need to respect the truth, the history, the reality, but you can't let history get in the way of the story. The worst mistake a writer can make in crafting historical fiction is to get too bogged down in history and not tell a story. This is a novel and the excitement of the plot needs to shine through.

You include the role that the First Nations played in the war. Why was it important to you to write about their contribution in **The Bully Boys?**

I read somewhere that the Battle of Beaver Dams was won by the First Nations people and they didn't get the credit they deserved. I wanted to give them that credit. Their bravery and honour in keeping their commitments were essential in turning the tide of war in our favour.

Do you think Lieutenant James FitzGibbon has received the recognition he deserved for his efforts in the war?

I believe that FitzGibbon is perhaps the single most important figure in our history in winning the War of 1812. Without him the Americans could have triumphed and this country might never have been created. Sir John A. Macdonald is the father of our country; FitzGibbon allowed this birth to take place.

Many people say that Canadian history is boring. What would your response be to that opinion?

Canadian history is exciting—the way it is often told is boring. Einstein said the universe isn't made of atoms but stories. Our job as writers is to tell the stories.

If you could transport yourself to another time in history, when would that be and why?

I'd like to be there at Camp X in Oshawa in 1941 and meet William Stephenson—the Man Called Intrepid— the man who inspired Ian Fleming to write James Bond. He was born in Winnipeg so I guess that James Bond should always speak with a Canadian accent.

What do you love the most about being an author?

I love everything. I get to explore, develop ideas, create, craft, write, travel, and follow my own heart wherever it wants to go.

The War of 1812

How It All Began

In 1812, Britain was involved in a long war with France and the Americans thought it was the perfect time to attack Canada. Upper and Lower Canada were under British protection, and with the British military forces busy in France, the Americans felt that a victory was guaranteed. They were tired of the British stopping American ships at sea, making sure they weren't sending goods to France or trying to find deserters from the British Navy. They also wanted to take over territory claimed by the First Nations, but this move was impossible when the Canadians were supporting Native rights and denying the Americans their expansion plans.

Who Was Involved?

The Canadian forces were greatly outnumbered by American fighters, so they had to use ingenuity, creativity, courage, and brute force to keep the enemy at bay. Canada prepared itself for war and called upon experienced British soldiers, Canadian volunteers, and First Nations allies to defend the borders. As the battles took place, valiant young heroes came to the forefront, creating a rich and lasting legacy. Isaac Brock, Tecumseh, Laura Secord, James FitzGibbon, and William Merritt are just some of the people who inspired Canadians during the war and continue to inspire them today.

While many of the battles took place on land, the Great Lakes also saw a great deal of action. Lakes Erie, Ontario, Huron, and Champlain had American and British fleets chasing one another from shore to shore. Whoever controlled the lakes had the upper hand in the war, as shipping troops and ammunition by boat was the quickest way to get the badly needed supplies to the awaiting forces.

Who Won?

Throughout the war, cities, towns, and forts were taken over by one side of the conflict, only to be retaken by the opposing side during another battle. The British and Canadian forces even made it all the way to Washington, where they burned the White House and every other government building. Both Canada and America have claimed victory regarding this war, but the outcome was not so clear-cut.

When the Treaty of Ghent was signed, all land and territory taken by an enemy force was restored to its original countries before the war. All prisoners were released and things generally went back to the way they were. The Canadians, however, were able to defend their country from invaders, which created an immense amount of national pride. It was the First Nations people who lost much in this war. Despite their efforts and sacrifices, the Treaty of Ghent did nothing to secure their territory and as years passed, they were further removed from their traditional lands.

Cool Things to Know

Laura Secord. The chocolate shop?

Yes, it's true. The chocolate shops that you can find all across Canada are named after the Canadian heroine. Frank P. O'Connor opened his first shop in 1913 on Yonge Street in Toronto, Ontario, naming it after Secord because of her loyalty and courage.

The White Truce Flag

When you were reading the story, did you wonder why Tommy and FitzGibbon were able to walk out to talk to the enemy forces by carrying a white flag? The origins of the white flag can be traced back hundreds of years. It is recognized around the world that when a white flag is flown, the person bearing it cannot be attacked or captured. But what if you want to surrender and you don't have a flag? Well, a t-shirt or handkerchief can also be used and then waved so that the opposing side can see that you are not armed and wish to surrender or speak to them in peace.

The Use of Muskets

In the War of 1812, many soldiers used muskets as weapons and wars were fought very differently from how they happen today. A soldier had to follow these steps before he could fire a musket: first he loaded it with gunpowder, and then he loaded a musket ball, followed by paper, to stop the powder and ball from falling out. The soldier then used a ramrod to push everything down the muzzle. All in all, it could take about 20 seconds to get ready to fire each shot.

Snail Mail

News travelled slowly in 1812, including the information that Britain had agreed to get rid of the laws that the United States objected to. Two days before US Congress decided to declare war, a message was sent across the ocean from Britain but it took several weeks before it reached land. By this time, the war was in full swing.

In addition, the Treaty of Ghent, which was the peace treaty that ended the war, was signed 15 days before the Battle of New Orleans. If this news had arrived faster, many lives could have been saved since this battle was one of the deadliest of the war.

The Wounded

The field hospitals, like where Tommy's father was found, were often dirty and depressing places. Unfortunately, there were no painkillers or anesthetics to help the wounded soldiers. The only thing they received was a drink of whiskey and then they bit down on a piece of leather to deal with the pain.

Though doctors in the war did their best to help the soldiers, amputation was often used for those with broken bones or serious wounds.

The Green Tigers

In 1813, Lieutenant James FitzGibbon handpicked 50 members for this special unit, who were trained to hunt down and capture US soldiers who were looting and burning farms. Trained in guerilla warfare, the Green Tigers sometimes wore green uniforms so they could camouflage themselves or wore disguises to trick the enemy.

Masters of Deception

FitzGibbon wasn't the only one who tried to fool American soldiers. Charles-Michel de Salaberry, a French-Canadian colonel, asked his First Nation allies to run through the forest surrounding the battleground whooping and hollering so that it sounded like there were many more men than there were in reality. He also had some men appear in their red coats, only to hide again and reappear in white coats. They simply turned them inside out and the Americans thought they were another regiment.

The 104th Regiment (New Brunswick)

While the fighting lessened during the winter months, those defending Canada felt that there would be a powerful assault from the Americans in the spring. Reinforcements were needed to help defend Upper Canada, so on February 16, 1813, members of the 104th regiment set out from Fredericton and marched—sometimes in snowshoes—all the way to Kingston, Ontario. On this epic journey they covered 1125 km in 52 days! They took part in many battles after their arrival and their participation showed how important it was for the provinces to join together and be united as one country.

What Does That Mean?

militia—the military force made up of civilians who were called to help the regular army when they needed reinforcements. Often, the members of the militia were not properly trained and had no uniforms or equipment.

long in the tooth—old. This phrase comes from the idea that as animals get older, their teeth continue to grow.

halfpence—a British coin that was the value of half a penny. Back in 1812, prices for goods were very low so you could buy something for less than a penny!

cavalry—soldiers who traditionally ride into battle on horses.

musket—a long firearm used by members of the infantry.

sympathizer—someone who supports the political ideas of a certain party. There were people in Canada who were American sympathizers, which means they wanted America to win the war. In the same way, there were British sympathizers who lived in America.

truce—an agreement between two opposing sides to stop fighting. A truce can be for a short or long period of time.